The Faster You Break

Riley Morgen Series Number One

Fletcher Felix

For those who are satiated by the darkest truths of human kind, unafraid to welcome the darkness inside…and those who beckon the darkness to play.

Prologue: Him

Mindlessly staring at the sole street lamp on this block, I wait patiently on the first floor of a parking garage. Tonight, I am on the hunt for number 241. I wish I could say that it would be a relaxing blood bath type of night for me, but this is work related. It must be a special occasion for the old man, ordering high quality merchandise instead of his typical type; a twenty-dollar suck and fuck special. He's always been more of a quantity over quality type of guy, more concerned about saving a dollar, I suppose. Tonight, his request specifically stated, 'the type of girl you would be proud to bring home to your mother'.

It's a shame really, that she'll be dead within the week.

It is nearly that time of the morning when the runners begin trickling to the sidewalks, society's standards of beauty forcing a certain type of woman to be among them. Just the type of product I am looking for.

And I, will be waiting for her.

Chapter One: Riley Morgen

The days of unpacking ahead of me feel so daunting that I already want to just ignore it completely. How long could I feign blindness to a maze of cardboard that cuts the square footage of my cabin in half? I'm actually quite confident I could impress even myself with this feat. Instead of entertaining the idea any longer, I decided to give in for the night and figure out a meal instead. I take the gurgling in my stomach as a thank you and grab the keys to my SUV.

When I bought this vehicle a few years ago, I remember having a hard time parallel parking in front of my townhouse in the city. The parking spaces were so tiny and everyone is packed in like a can of sardines. I questioned if the city life was not compatible with an oversized SUV but I wanted both. The mix of the way I grew up with the introduction of my adult life in a city. I never regretted getting it, except that first night knowing that all my neighbors were absolutely peeking out their windows thoroughly impressed with my lack of parallel parking skills. Why is it a thousand times harder to complete a simple task when you know judging eyes are glued to your performance? I may have had zero experience with parallel parking but I was no stranger to handling a vehicle. While it may have stood out in the city, the SUV seems to blend into the crowd here in Bearpoint.

Bearpoint is a nature lover's paradise. Adjacent to the Appalachian Mountains means endless hiking trails to explore and more wildlife per square foot than human beings.

This is exactly what I need. After about fifteen minutes of driving, without making a single deviation, I arrive in the heart of this tiny town. A single road lined on both sides with twelve businesses containing everything the residents of Bearpoint need. Perfect for the person who can never decide what to eat, I park my car in front of the only choice my life now offers, a cabin style standalone building with a small stone and wood sign announcing itself as The Conway.

As a single person, sitting at the bar of restaurants has become the norm. On my better days, I enjoyed the company of the other patrons and bartender. On my worst days, I would often get food to go and stop at a liquor store on the walk home. As much as my routine will change leaving the bustling city life, I most look forward to changing my own toxic habits that I picked up being so submersed in city life and an even more toxic employer.

"Hello there, you're new to town, right? That cop that moved into the old Jenkins place, right?" the smiling bartender inquires.

There was a time in my life when being referred to as 'that cop' would have filled me with pride for all the work I have put in. Today, I inwardly cringe knowing that I have moved to a small town that feels a world away to start my entire life over and the only reputation I have here is the title of a career I left behind.

I swallow down all the contempt threatening to spew from my throat and muster as casual a smile as possible. "Yes, I bought the cabin from Mr. Jenkins. I used to work in law enforcement, but I actually left the career. I'm here for a fresh start and to reconnect with nature."

3

Probably the most rehearsed answer in my repertoire but better to fluff than to pull this stranger into the spiraling quicksand filling my brain at the mere mention of policing.

There is nothing worse in this career than being employed by a toxic department. A toxic department can strip you of happiness and your love of the career. I can tell you this first hand. The hardest part of leaving a destructive department is the overwhelming sense of relief coupled with suddenly being treated like an outsider. The officers you thought were your friends for years change their tune quickly when they realize you are no longer willingly drinking the poison fed by the administration. The administration may be pouring the glasses, but every officer that takes a sip and passes it to the next is just as complicit in the toxic environment itself. I drank heartily for eight years. I couldn't do it anymore. I wanted to love this career again. I wanted to help when someone is drowning instead of just treading water myself.

Leaving the department was a necessity, but the change of scenery is a luxury. For the last eight years, I lived and worked in a violent city environment. A city never truly shuts down. Late nights bring addicts and sex workers wandering the streets, club patrons lining the sidewalks, desperate criminals making life altering decisions and police sirens lulling the rest of the city to sleep. Admittingly, after eight years of policing in an environment like this, I have become cynical. There have been many adrenaline-fueled moments in my career that are envied by uninvolved officers. I have seen and handled things that no human being should be subjected to…and gotten paid for it. I have changed both for the worst and for the better. I have been miserable with my career choice and absolutely elated by it. I learned that this is how most officers feel. The roll call room is often filled with vile feelings and inhumane jokes masking mountains of built-up trauma and long-standing grudges. Still, every person there puts on the uniform and spends the shift adding to the buildup. It is a sick cycle that borders an addiction.

As the waves of cynicism have ebbed and waned over the years, I have had both moments of absolute clarity and of zero visibility. Three months ago, brought a wave of clarity that once seen, I could not turn back. I decided to uproot my home, change my scenery and become reintroduced to myself outside of the title of police officer. It felt so freeing in the moment, so unavoidable once the seed of realization had been planted. I just didn't expect the wave of an aftermath that threatens to drown you once you finally leave.

"Well, if you're looking to reconnect with nature, you certainly found the right place to do it."

The bartender chuckles, handing me a one-sided menu and continuing, "I'm Jack Bennett. Let me know if you need anything, I know this place can be an adjustment."

"Thanks Jack, I'm Riley. I really just need a burger…and a draft."

Chapter Two: Riley Morgen

A few days of unpacking has done little for my mental state but a sense of accomplishment begins to settle as I break down the last empty box. I need this. I need to get away from that uniform and reset my brain…reset my life. There is such a stigma to leaving the brotherhood of policing, you feel as if you've lost everything. The coworkers that became family, the purpose that guided your life decisions, and so many unique skills that are only exercised by being active in this career. It's a career that changes you in both positive and negative ways. I, unfortunately, was a member of a department that oozed noxious gas. I need to find myself out here in regular life and figure out how to let go of everything that is mentally drowning me.

I grab a cold beer and head for the front porch. I may not have an opportunity to people watch here in Bearpoint, but this view is entertaining in a way I didn't even know I needed. Directly in front of me, some odd miles in the distance, sits an enormous mountain covered in a blanket of deep green pine trees. I can't help but wonder what life is out there. There must be hundreds of species of animals coexisting in their own ecosystem, completely unimpressed with their human neighbors. Each day of their lives consumed by nothing more than survival. The meaning of survival varying greatly for each creature, but all coming down to one simple thing. I can relate to that mindset. An orange ember of a sun sits immediately atop the mountain's peak, acting as the cherry

6

atop the whole view. It is mesmerizing and humbling to be such a small piece of this world. I want to be absorbed by this world and forget any others I have known.

As the sun is beginning to set, slowly disappearing behind the mountain, I am seated on my porch steps enjoying my third beer. The mountain air is beginning to feel crisp and cool as the sun sets, bringing needed refreshment to my skin after sitting in direct sunlight for the last hour. I have been so consumed with unpacking lately that I haven't truly explored my own property yet. I get up, wiping off my jeans, and set off down the stairs walking toward the back side of my new property. The cabin is surrounded on all sides by endless pines and oaks, some young and some older than any living human. The air is so heavily purified that I feel slightly light headed. Whether my city ridden body is responding to the pollution free air, or the change in elevation, I decide it's for the best that I sit down.

The earth feels cool and soft beneath me, pulsing in and out of my outstretched fingers. For the hundreds of creatures roaming my direct area, the forest has a surprising stillness. A unique understanding of every creature's place and purpose. After a few peacefully deep breaths, I am mentally preparing to get back to my feet when I see movement out of the corner of my eye. Swiftly looking up, my eye focuses deep in the woods. A distance from me, there is movement through the dark, dense forest. I still completely, feeling exposed in the open wood line. A hot fear burns deep in my belly as my brain processes the figure is human. The shadowy movement is impossible to judge any distinguishing features, even gender or clothing. The movement is consistent. Slow and methodical. Almost floating above the root laden earth. I slowly brace my hands on the ground, realizing how vulnerable I am, readying myself to better my position. I glance down to scan for any items near me that could be used should a fight occur. A fist sized rock or sharp stick would do the trick. The momentary scan complete, I glance back toward the figure to discover that they are gone. I quickly scan the area and get to my feet, scanning again. My scans come up empty and I quickly head toward the cabin, listening intently for any snap of a twig or the pound of hurried feet behind me. The stillness of the forest is heavy in its return.

Chapter Three: Her "Number 241"

It's so cold. I try to sit up but I can barely move. My head is throbbing and every inch of my body hurts. Where am I? The ground is so hard and cold, I flex my fingers against it and feel the tips of my nails crack against metal. Every inch of me feels brittle, broken. I have to sit up. I have to go home. As I try to force myself in a seated position, my head is met with a hard rattling metal. Fighting against a spinning dizziness, I blindly reach around me, hoping to gather my bearings. I am met with small metal bars surrounding my body.

Nausea washes over me as the realization settles in…I am in a cage. I become suddenly aware of a sharp pain in my ankle. Involuntarily grabbing for the pain, my fingers are met by cold steel. What the fuck? What is on me? My fingers tracing the metal in the dark, I am wearing a large metal cuff around my ankle, there is a chain attached. The chain is leading up into the endless darkness. What the fuck is happening to me? My brain is spinning, the panic is setting in. I can barely think, my head is pounding. Barely speak, my throat raw. I try to clear my throat but I barely make a sound. My throat feels caked with the taste of rusty metal.

"Help." I whisper, scarcely audible.

"Help." I try to project my voice, but the rusty metal coating my throat has left me so hoarse.

"Help." I muster in a voice that sounds nothing like my own.

9

I am caged, surrounded by a cold unrelenting darkness that is threatening to consume me.

"No one will hear you." A hiss from the darkness.

I am caged, surrounded by a cold unrelenting darkness that is threatening to consume me...

and I am not alone.

Chapter Four: Him

You would think with the obsession this world has with true crime and the amount of information accessible on the internet, we would have a hardcore batch of serial killers running around freely adding to their body counts. If you know all the ways you could be caught, it is simple to evade detection. It is so black and white, a literal outline for the wicked. Unfortunately, very few people are like me. The information is out there but you still have to be something special to both please your most vile desires and be intelligent enough to control yourself. It is an art...and I am an artist. Let's just say no one was surprised when I made my pleasure into my business. I imagine this is what whores feel like. The pleasure of a fuck while lining the pockets.

I've been supplying the old man for years. I mean, look at the guy. No woman is willingly getting in a car with that meth mouth son-of-a-bitch. He's grotesque. Couple that with the fact that his house emanates an odor that only a carnivore just risen from a winter long hibernation would find appealing. It's a mix of iron and burnt flesh. I get the iron. I wasn't always so clean with my knife work, slicing a person up like a Christmas ham produces that deep iron rich smell...I was craving it for weeks after that first one. Now the burnt flesh. I know the smell...but that one is not a part of my repertoire. I could understand a lesser man knowing the smell well, burning the evidence rather than putting in the effort to keep your work clean. Maybe he burns the bodies to get rid of 'em...or maybe the old man is eating these chicks. What the fuck do I know. As long as he keeps paying me, I'll keep finding his girls.

Chapter Five: Riley Morgen

I wake the next morning to a knock at my front door that makes me nearly jump out of my skin. Well, I jumped out of the bed anyway...and ate the wall in a tangle of blankets that rendered my legs immobile. Heart pounding, my first thought is of the figure I saw in the woods yesterday. I holster my Glock and strap it to my sweatpants before approaching the door. I glance out the front window and see a familiar face waiting impatiently, raising her hand to knock again.

Before I can even fully open the door, my mother rushes inside.

"Riley Rose Morgen. Why have I not received an invite to your new home? I have to surprise my own child just to see the place?"

"Good morning, Mom."

"Good morning my little ray of sunshine. Are we going to stand in the doorway all day or do I get a tour of the place?"

As I walk my mom through the one thousand square foot cabin, I listen to the thinly veiled criticisms that I've grown to know mask her worry about me. Prior to starting my career in law enforcement, my relationship with my mother was extremely close. Yet another side effect of the career...relationships suffer and your view of people becomes jaded. Even the people you love. I don't blame her for worrying. I've never delved into the details of everything I've seen...everything I've survived. But no matter how hard I tried to fight it, it all changed me. I don't think anyone leaves this career unscathed.

"Can I get you something to drink, Mom?"

"Iced tea of course. So, what is the game plan here?" She gestures broadly to the small space, made even smaller by cardboard boxes I have yet to throw away.

"Well. I'm taking some much-needed time and relaxation in nature. I'm hoping to rediscover some of my passions and let that guide me into the next career move for me." Yet another bullshit answer pulled out of my line up.

"I'm glad you left honey, I really am. And I do believe you need a break, but I'm worried you're not taking a break… you're running."

It's hard not to roll my eyes. This is a conversation I expected, but it still feels so taxing.

"Mom. I'm not running from anything. I just need to reset."

"You could reset at home. You didn't need to come out to the mountains and hide from everyone that loves you. I know you are struggling with everything that happened at work, and you really need to talk to someone."

I couldn't fight the eye roll this time. The last thing I need right now is to open up to some therapist who can't understand the first thing about standing over a dead body, staring at chunks of brain while a river of blood inches closer to your boots. Some therapist who can't understand what it's like climbing into an attic to find a teenage girl hanging from the rafters, neck broken so inhumanely that the image will never leave your mind. Some therapist who can't understand how it feels to leave a call like that, only to go to the next like nothing ever happened. Only to have to get into a gunfight and pray that you go home with your life.

14

Don't get me wrong, I am not opposed to therapy. I am not opposed to getting help. But at this point, I can't imagine delving into the thousand worsts of my days and having anyone besides another officer understand what I need them to understand. I don't believe that anyone else could understand me at this point. And the reality is, officers don't help each other through these feelings. They lean so deeply into a dark sense of humor and detachment that a typical roll call would shock most civilians. A career in law enforcement teaches you that coping is stuffing everything down, wrapped in the neat little bow made of fucked up humor. Pain and feelings are weakness, and officers are not weak.

"Mom, I will talk to someone when I need to talk. The best thing for me right now is to reset and rediscover what I want for myself. If that includes therapy, I will do that. I can make those decisions without you stressing over it."

"Darling, I will always stress over you. It's literally in my job description."

Chapter Six: Riley Morgen

The past few weeks have been filled with nothing but nature and solitude, and damn does it feel good. I'm starting to feel settled into this place but I admit that the lack of adrenaline spikes is a new experience for me. Is there such a thing as missing chaos? Damn, maybe I am as messed up in the head as my mom thinks. Instead of trying to crack open that egg, I decide it's best for me to get some nature therapy.

Years ago, I hated running with a passion that ran deeper than my bones. The police academy forced that out of me. The first few months were absolutely brutal. I dreaded every day knowing that running miles, in formation and cadence, was inevitable. The reality I had to accept was that the hatred affected nothing and no one but the person drowning in that feeling. *Me.*

Every pound on the pavement, every pain, every struggle, was nothing more than weakness leaving my body. The instructors screaming that statement more times than anyone cared to count really started the brainwashing early... *pain is weakness leaving your body.* The ironic thing of it all, was acceptance of the inevitable led me to finding a true passion for the thing I believed I hated. As I run now, the beads of sweat dripping down my forehead drain the stress from my mind. My mind is filled with nothing but the present moment; breathe, foot pounding, sweat rolling. *Breathe, pound, roll. Breathe, pound, roll.*

As I lose myself to the pattern of my run, I let my eyes soak in the beauty encompassing me. It is an entirely different world, just forty miles from the city of Minwall, and I feel like I could give myself completely to its glory. I am snapped back from my daydreaming by the figure of a man running about a quarter of a mile in front of me. He is too far ahead to see any features, but is wearing a black t-shirt and dark green joggers. I silently criticize his running gait and imagine that I would win any race paired against this guy, chuckling to myself at how the police academy created such a competitive streak in me. I should try to catch up and see if I could make a new running friend, but I don't feel quite ready to put myself out there like that. Solitude will suit me just fine for a while.

Surrounded by pine trees, feet gliding across the dirt running path, I begin to slow to a walking pace and take in the beauty around me. The pines, the mountains, the peace feels never-ending. The cool mountain breeze slowly drying my sweat, I decide to turn around and begin a walk back to the cabin. As I appreciate the gentle warmth of the sun on my wet skin and fresh air in my lungs, a glint catches my eye. Two feet off the dirt path, a glimmer within the fallen pine needles. Scooping my fingers deep into the brush, I lift my hand and gently skim through the foliage. Pine needles scatter and a small golden locket remains in my palm. I turn the heart over in my hand, looking for any unique descriptors. It looks worn, but not old, just well loved. Someone will definitely miss this. I glance up, looking for the runner I just saw, thinking maybe he just dropped it. The trail around me has stilled again, no sign of the runner, just me and the cool gentle breeze. My fingernail searching for an edge that can be

17

opened, I attempt to pry the two sides, hopeful that a picture will reveal more information about the owner. No luck. I slide the locket into the pocket of my running shorts, planning to turn it into the local sheriff's office the next time I'm in town.

_____ **** _____

After arriving home, I take a cool shower and put on sweatpants, a t-shirt and my most comfortable fuzzy socks. I am a sucker for a good pair of socks. This particular pair are red and black flannel, covered in a luxurious fuzz that envelops my feet in a velvety nirvana. My feet are especially appreciative after that trail run. In the last few years, the news has been a source of stress and frustration for me but a few weeks with near zero human interaction has put me in a place of craving information. I plop down on the couch and turn the television to the local news station. I say local, but this town has nothing going on. I have to admit that fact is a relief to me after being a city cop where there is always too much going on.

As a feel-good story about a charity collecting canned goods meeting a new goal is coming to an end, the attractive blonde newscaster's face quickly shifts. The signal of a serious story to come.

"Breaking news coming to our desk tonight involving a young woman missing out of Minwall."

As the newscaster speaks, an image pops up on the screen of a young woman who appears to be in her early twenties. The image is set outdoors, a large pine behind her right shoulder and the sun beaming down on her smiling face.

18

The smile comes from someone who genuinely enjoys life. So much innocence behind it, a life not yet tainted by darkness. It's interesting the way a smile can convey so much. The way the lips turn ever so slightly can indicate lies, discomfort, or even sadness. It's often said that people can hide anything behind a smile, but I've always believed that the smallest, almost imperceptible, movements in one's expression so rarely lie. This is the smile of a woman who is basking in what life has offered her. Her hair, a sun kissed shade of golden-brown cascades down her shoulders, gleaming in the sunlight as if competing with those perfect set of pearly whites. The hazel eyes staring straight into the screen show no sign of worry, no sign of a troubled future to come.

As I remove myself from my assessment of the photo, the newscaster continues, "Twenty-one-year-old Julia Preston was last seen leaving her Minwall apartment early Saturday morning. Friends say that she typically runs in Lawson Park on the west end of the city. It is believed that was her destination. Authorities are asking that anyone who may have seen the young woman contact the Minwall Police Department with information."

Ugh, the Minwall Police Department. As much as I want to roll my eyes at the thought of my old department, I suppress the urge. It is surprising the number of people that are reported missing every day in a large city. The majority have left of their own accord and return home completely unharmed. The fact that I am seeing this story on the news leaves a dark pit in my stomach. The department has an entire team of detectives that work solely on missing person's cases. As an officer, I typically took the report and never heard

19

about it again. The individual would be located before the report even had an investigator assigned, most of the time. This young woman must be in actual danger if the department is turning to media coverage.

The city has enough shootings every week, that their name is never left out of the news. I highly doubt that they would add to that type of exposure unless there were no other options. It is yet another disgusting reality of that police department…the public image is so overwhelmingly negative and the crime stats are at the forefront of all budget negotiations with the city. In order to mitigate this, the department changes the way crimes are designated for the statistics. There are so many homicides that they began categorizing them as death investigations to avoid adding another homicide to the stats. It suddenly looks like homicide numbers have gone down, yet the death investigation numbers are higher than ever before.

I do not know anything about this investigation…the circumstances, the interviews with friends and family, the theories swirling. I do know one thing…Julia Preston is in danger.

Chapter Seven: Julia Preston "Number 241"

I am not alone. A wave of nausea burns my stomach and I think I am going to be sick. I am not alone. I think my heart is going to burst through my chest. I am trapped. I am someone's victim. I am going to die. I am going to die like a caged animal. Oh God, please save me. Oh God, my mom. I can't leave my mom. Images of my family begin flashing through my mind at rapid speed… I can't do this to them. I can't die. Oh my God, am I going to die? The panic is consuming me, burning hot tears are streaming down my face. I can't die like this.

That's it.

I can't die like this.

I won't die like this.

I can't let myself fall apart.

I have to fight this.

Every piece of me is aching with a pain I never knew existed. I have to keep my mind in check. It's all I have right now. I begin to look around, trying to force my eyes to give me any information. The darkness is so consuming, I can't even see my hand in front of my face. I reach my hand out, feeling every bar of icy, rough metal surrounding me. I slowly work my hand down every bar, looking for any weak spots, anything I can use to my advantage. I don't even feel a door…how did I get in this thing? Okay. Okay, I have to keep myself together. If I am going to make it out of this cage alive, I have to stay calm and use my brain. A thought occurs to me

21

blurred by my initial panic…who is here with me? I search my mind for the voice; I try to replay what I just heard. *No one will hear you.* The terror those words rose in me blinded me to one realization…it was a woman's voice.

"Who are you?" I whisper into the darkness.

The silence that fills the room leaves me listening to my own heartbeat. It is still pounding in my chest, even if I have gotten some sense of control over my mind.

"Who is there?" I managed to squeak out slightly louder than my previous whisper.

"I am a nobody…just like you."

The words bite with a sorrow I have never felt in my life.

"My name is Julia Preston. I am not a nobody. I have a good life; I am not a nobody." I repeat this for good measure. I have never felt like a perfect person, but I have never felt so low as to call myself a nobody. I will not do it now. No one can take who I am from me.

"I used to think I was someone too…but here…I am nothing. You are nothing, Julia. The sooner you accept that, the easier your fate will be." The voice surrounded by darkness is so filled with despair, I can feel it in the air. It is heavy and sticky on my skin, even with the chills I feel deep inside my body, this is hot…and sickening.

"Are you caged too?" I decide not to push for her identity, and instead try to gain as much information as I can.

"We all are." She states so matter of fact. As if it is nothing. As if it isn't an earth-shattering statement.

"We?" The disbelief and fear now impossible to hide from my shaking voice.

Chapter Eight: Him

There's something about watching your own art being admired on a stage. It's the sole reason I watch the news. I don't give a fuck about the sob bullshit stories this blond bimbo feeds the idiot masses. I accepted it years ago...I am surrounded by a world of idiots. I am the lion watching a mass of gazelle unsuspectingly filling their mouths with shit laced water. And all the while, I just laugh. I have never and will never be one of those drones. One who walks this earth marching the path that is forced upon you, dying surrounded by people who coexisted with you for so long that you believe there is some actual bond. Then calling that the dream. What a joke.

Finally, the bimbo is getting to the good stuff. As the picture of my latest gazelle covers the screen, I can't help but feel pride. *Hello, number 241, so good to see you again.* This is my handy work. This is my mark on the world. I admit she was a scrumptious one. The old man is lucky I didn't play with my prey before the delivery. Don't get me wrong, I wanted too, but I am a professional. I didn't make a name for myself fucking around with the product. The classic move of a gazelle wearing a lion's coat...get high on your own supply. Nah, I'm too good for that. I am pure bred beast through and through. This gazelle knew it. I was almost impressed. I've always been able to use my face and a mask of charm to ease any victim into truly believing I was safe. That moment when the realization of their new reality sets in...the memories make me nearly swell with excitement. It is so enticing; I began craving it. That moment when they knew that I was their God. That nothing else existed…nothing else could exist, but me. And I would not prove to be a merciful God, no, I would be the thing that their nightmares could not contain.

This gazelle was unusual. I knew she was attracted to me; I knew she wanted to believe I was safe…but the doubt never left her eyes. No, this one required a bit more work than my typical job. I reveled in it. I would never stoop so low as to call my work boring, but there have been lulls. Product like this brings me back to the true artistry. The true mastery of my craft…and myself. The hard work I have put in to honing this craft. The improvements I have made along the way to become a master. As I begin to reminisce about my most recent work, my phone begins to vibrate.

Ah, the work never ends.

Chapter Nine: Riley Morgen

I wake to the rising sun welcoming itself into my bedroom windows. Ugh, who invited you? I roll over, burying my head into my pillow, hoping to trick myself into sleep again. The last eight years of my life have existed only in the hours that people typically fill with sleep. Two months of living in this cabin and my circadian rhythm is slowly resetting. My mind is not quite on board just yet. I have always been a night owl, but law enforcement solidified that quirk. Maybe changing that habit is a good thing.

Begrudgingly, I force myself out of bed and head straight for the coffee maker. The interior of my new home is a classic log cabin, filled with an expanse of cedar and accents of fieldstone that once called the Appalachian Mountains home. They are now subjected to my company, and I am grateful for it. The nature constantly surrounding me has been a form of therapy for me. I have always been partial to homes that flaunt the natural materials of their area, though it had been such a rarity in my life while living in the city. The city streets are lined with cookie cutter townhomes, apartment buildings and parking garages towering in the sky. A flood of concrete and brick dulling the senses. I am beginning to feel more alive spending so much time surrounded by the living.

I decide to enjoy my coffee on the front porch so I can properly soak in the morning sun. There's something about the soft heat of the early sun that awakens the soul. I close my eyes, breathing deep, enjoying the cleanliness of the air and alluring scent of my coffee when I am struck with the sudden vision of Julia Preston. When I was a police officer, it became easy to mentally disconnect myself from the constant pain I would see on every call. People aren't inviting us into their world to celebrate their happy moments. We are only there for the worst moments of their lives. As a means of self-preservation, you learn early on in your career to disconnect from the human aspect of these moments. The families of victims bring the hardest moments to witness. At times they are losing someone who meant the world to them, in that loss their world is ceasing its existence. When a loved one is missing, it is a feeling of complete helplessness. The thoughts of what if…what if I tried harder…what if I had just done one thing different…would they still be here next to me? As the responding officer, the emotions behind these moments cannot exist. You are there with the sole purpose of help led by logic. Slowly, as I part myself from the career, I am getting floods of emotional realization. All the pain of those left behind in every tragic moment I bared witness to. I did not witness these moments with Julia's friends and family…why am I experiencing the emotions of moments I did not witness?

I can't help but feel this weight. I give over to the side of logic and decide to look at this case the way an investigator would view it. What do I know? Julia Preston was last seen four days ago. She is twenty-one years old, which can sometimes be a good indication that she may be safe with someone that she just hasn't introduced to her friends or family yet. A possibility, but without knowing more about the victim I can't say whether that is likely or not for Julia. Without the precious information her loved ones would provide the investigator; I can only speculate based on her photograph. She appears to be happy and full of life, no signs of negativity or deception in her expression. Her friends stated that she typically goes for a run in the west end of the city, Lawson Park. While the city is known for a high volume of violent crime, the west end of the city is a decent place to live. The majority of reported crime there is minor…noise complaints, larcenies, rarely anything violent in nature. The median home price is higher than the surrounding counties, but the plots are small. The options mostly consist of townhomes or condos. The majority of businesses in this area offer good jobs and expect candidates with college degrees. These factors typically attract young professionals. The news didn't release any information about Julia's career, but it seems likely that she falls into the category of a young professional. It was never specifically stated that she was seen in the park, so I assume police are unsure of whether she actually entered Lawson Park or not.

I would never wish myself back to the city, but I feel this pull for more information. Am I actually having withdrawals from a lack of insider information? Is that a thing? Similar to starting this career, ending it has left me with the realization that nothing prepares you for the way your life and mind change. Deep down, I know this decision is right for me. That doesn't stop the mental struggle, unfortunately. No, that will have to be solved in this moment with keeping busy. Draining the last of my coffee, I head inside to change my clothes and give my mind to the wonderful world of manual labor. Oh yes, the wild world of chopping firewood.

Chapter Ten: Riley Morgen

One week has passed since news broke of Julia Preston's disappearance. Despite my best efforts to distract my mind, I find myself glued to the news nightly desperate for any nugget of information. I'm like an addict waiting for her next fix. While my stores of firewood for winter are grateful for the excessive replenishment, I am left with a helpless feeling that has caused me to delve into an expanse of speculation. I can't imagine this being healthy and am well aware of my need for further distraction. Tonight, I give in to this need and decide to drive into town for dinner.

The Conway appears to be the heartbeat of this area, which I guess is not surprising when the town consists of twelve businesses total. Apparently, this is the place to be on a Saturday night, judging by the packed tables and buzz of laugher that hits me as I open the door. To my relief, there are a few empty barstools that beckon to me and I make a beeline straight for the bar. I glance up at the mirror lining the wall behind the liquor bottles. After so many years in law enforcement, it feels strange to see my chestnut brown hair falling down my shoulders, instead of tied in a tight bun on top of my head. I'm pleasantly surprised to see that there are no bags under my eyes, a welcome byproduct of actually sleeping I assume, and my pale skin seems to have a bit of a glow. As I sit, I am immediately greeted by Jack, who apparently is the only bartender crazy enough to believe an area like this is a great place for a man of his trade to buy a home.

"Riley! I was starting to think my ugly mug was keeping you away from this place!" He places a coaster and menu in front of me as he speaks.

"Well, it hasn't made me lose my appetite yet so I'd say you're in the clear." I taunted.

His mug is not, in fact, ugly. Not even a little. I'm sure Jack has his pick of whatever limited number of single women exist in a small mountain town. If I had to guess, Jack is in his late twenties or early thirties. In the two times I have seen him he has worn the same long sleeve black button-down shirt, sleeves rolled up the forearms. As if fearing being seen as too professional, he couples it with a pair of blue jeans. The shirt is just loose enough on his tall frame to hide any protruding muscle, though based on the cut of his forearms I imagine that he is not lacking in that department. A strong stubble-free jaw, easy going smile and bright emerald eyes are nothing to shy away from either. Plus, I've always been a sucker for a dark-haired man. Yeah, not a speckle of ugly on that mug.

Jack lets out a hardy laugh and displays that easy smile. "Then let me get you something to munch on. What you in the mood for?"

"At the risk of sounding too classy, I'll have a burger. Extra fries...and a draft, please."

There goes that smile again. "My pleasure."

As I sit waiting for my food, I take a moment to soak in my surroundings. First the people, some laughing, some deep in conversation, some glued to the few television screens scattered around the restaurant...none a threat. This is a habit I hope to break. I hope to stop assessing every being around me for the level of threat they pose. It is a tiring habit. The building itself seems to be typical to the area, filled with wood and stone. In the back corner is a fireplace surrounded by a stone covered wall all the way to the celling. I look forward to sitting by that fire sipping something fiery this winter.

Jack pulls me from my appreciation of possible future plans by placing a ginormous plate filled with a burger and extra fries in front of me. "If you need more fries, let me know."

This earns a laugh out of me, "If I need more fries, I will be too ashamed to admit it to anyone, even myself."

After stuffing the first fry into my mouth unashamedly, I swallow so hard I near choke. My attention is caught by a familiar face on the television screen above me.

"Jack! Turn this up! Hurry!" The excitement in my voice is coupled by my waving finger, pointing to the television screen.

Detective Nicolas Ares stands behind a podium, dressed in a pressed blue suit, looking solemn. Detective Ares is well known within the Minwall Police Department, with a stellar reputation. He has sixteen years of solving cases at a yearly rate that most officers will never meet over an entire career. Despite such an impressive record, no officer is perfect. There will always be cases that go unsolved, no matter what powerhouse gives it their all. An officer can only work with what they are given during an investigation.

Beyond his many professional achievements, he is a good man. That is a quality that not all officers are strong enough to hold onto. He has managed to never falter in his best qualities and to never allow another human to change his heart. For these reasons, Detective Ares working on a case means that another detective has exhausted all routes. While that would be a deterrent to most other detectives, Ares takes it as an exciting challenge. I always imagined him as a kid, solving mystery books before the killer was even introduced as a character.

"As of today, I will be the detective working the missing persons case of Julia Preston. For those of you who are uninformed of the case, Julia Preston is a twenty-one-year-old woman residing in the west end of the city of Minwall. Julia was last seen ten days ago in the area of Lawson Park. She was wearing a light blue, short sleeve, dry fit running top and black mesh shorts. We have no reason to believe that Julia would have disappeared of her own accord. For this reason, we again ask the public to contact the Minwall Police Department with any tips or possible sightings. Regardless of how insignificant the information may seem; it could be key to our investigation."

A wave of nausea washes over me. A gaping pit of despair opening wide inside my belly threatening to swallow me whole. Before I can realize what I am doing, I am on my feet rushing for the door. I clutch my chest, feeling my lungs tighten. Am I having a panic attack?

"Riley! Wait! Where are you going?"

I hear Jack from somewhere behind me but I can't stop now. I need to get away from this. I need this feeling to stop.

"Riley! What about your food?"

————————— **** —————————

As soon as I rush through my front door, I slam it closed, fumbling with the locks. I slide down to the floor, breathing deep. *We have no reason to believe that Julia would have disappeared of her own accord.* I can hear Ares' words pounding in my head. They know she was abducted and they have no leads. Detective Ares taking over the case tells me that much. The thing I felt in my gut all along has finally bubbled to the surface. For all the sickness I feel, for all the distance I have tried to put between myself and this career, I can't ignore the severity of this situation.

I once again find myself sitting in front of the television watching the eleven o'clock news repeat of Detective Ares' press conference. This time, having nowhere to run from, I see the clip in its entirety. As the end of the clip approaches, new photos of Julia Preston appear on the screen. The final photo, Julia in a flowing green sundress catches my attention. A golden glint sparkles from Julia's otherwise bare collarbone. I jump up from my seat on the couch and scurry across the room, face inches from the television screen. It's a necklace. A golden locket.

I run into my bedroom, grabbing for the pile of dirty laundry thrown in the corner of the room. Tossing piece by piece across the floor I find my workout clothes from my run last week. Frantically squeezing the pockets, I feel the hard lump. My breathing hard and too loud for my own ears, I slowly pull the necklace from the pocket. A golden locket. Turning the locket over in my hands, studying for anything I missed on first inspection, I find nothing but the same simple gold locket I saw one week ago. I run my fingers along the seam sealing the two sides of the heart together and again try to pull it open. No luck. Is this thing stuck together or is the seam just for show? Is this Julia Preston's locket? I'm sure a million girls have golden lockets. Is this really something specific to her? Am I holding a key to this case thinking this is nothing of significance? *Regardless of how insignificant the information may seem; it could be key to our investigation.* I again hear Ares' words replaying in my head. The officer in me knows that it could be nothing…or it could be everything.

Chapter Eleven: Riley Morgen

I barely slept. An ocean of restless energy consumed me all night, wondering if that locket could have any connection to Julia Preston. At least no sleep means no nightmares. I tried to remind myself that there is no obvious definitive connection. Despite the attempt, I only became more convinced that I am holding some unknown key. For that reason, I find myself standing in the lobby of the Bearpoint Sheriff's Office. The differences between my experiences of a police precinct and this department's only building are stark. Not that I expected any different, but I imagine policing here might actually be a pleasant experience. That, or incredibly boring.

Two men clad in deep brown deputy uniforms appear from the back room. The first, a sixty something, heavy-set man with thinning gray hair dons a gold star shaped badge on his chest and an exasperated look on his wrinkled face. I've annoyed him before I even opened my mouth…wish I could say that's a first. The second deputy, a thirty something, fitness conscious man with dark eyes and hair to match. His expression appears friendly and open, adding to his strikingly handsome face. This man dons a silver star shaped badge on his chest. Okay, clearly grumpy is in charge here.

"Can I help you, Miss?" Grumpy asks.

I smile sweetly at Grumpy's sour face. "Riley Morgen. I'm sure you've heard about the young woman missing out of Minwall, Julia Preston."

34

"Everyone has, Miss Morgen. We all watch the news. Any information you may think you have should be reported to the Minwall Police Department. You can just give them a call." Grumpy begins to turn, ready to brush me off that quickly.

"I understand but I believe this may involve the Bearpoint Sheriff's Office as well. Last week, I went for a run on Binkin Trail and I found a necklace. I picked it up, planning to bring it here to turn it into lost and found. Last night while I was watching the latest press conference on the news, I saw a photograph of Julia Preston and I believe she is wearing the same necklace in the photograph."

I try my best to be succinct with my facts, and not let the urgency surging in my veins make me sound emotional. A man like Grumpy is clearly not very interested in what a woman has to say…especially one he deems as 'emotional'. I know his type well, unfortunately.

The look of skepticism on Grumpy's face is enough to force me to mentally restrain myself from slapping it right off of him.

"Miss Morgen. Is there some unique feature to this necklace that makes you believe that?"

"Well, no. Not any specific feature, but it is a golden locket that appears the same as the photo. I realize there is nothing proving it is exact but I think it is worth looking into and I thought I should inform you because it is in your jurisdiction."

"I'm sure you're just overthinking a coincidence, Miss Morgen."

I know enough about officers that come in with preconceived notions to try to push this issue any further. The first indication of an officer who thinks words out of anyone's mouth but their own is a waste of airwaves.

"Well, I won't waste any more of your time with my overthinking coincidences then. I appreciate your time."

At that, Grumpy's lips curled into an obviously fake forced smile and he turns immediately, heading back to the room he appeared from. Clearly, thankful to get rid of the meddling overthinker. As I watch him leave, a figure out of the corner of my eye catches my attention. Deputy handsome stares at me unmoved from his spot. I smile, subconsciously sending him the "I'm sorry your boss is a total shit head" signals.

"I'm Deputy May and that was Sheriff Marks. I'm sorry about that...he can be a bit brash."

"Brash isn't quite the word I would have used, but I appreciate you saying that."

This earned an appreciative smile so I continue, "I realize I'm not offering any hard evidence here but I do believe it is worth looking into. And I will call Detective Ares with MPD as well, but I assumed it was worth informing the jurisdiction possible evidence was found in."

"You talk like a cop, Miss Riley Morgen. You have a badge hidden somewhere?"

I laugh, appreciative of Deputy May's easy-going nature. "If I did, I would have been shoving it in Sheriff Marks' face after that conversation. I used to be an officer with Minwall Police Department. I left a few months ago and came here to get away from it...it appears to have followed me here."

"Well for what it's worth Miss Riley...I think you could be onto something. I mean, that would be one heck of a coincidence to find the exact same necklace right when Miss Julia went missing. It's worth lookin' into."

"Will you help me?" I ask, suddenly hopeful that I may have an ally here. The sudden change in Deputy May's face brings my hope to a swift end.

Looking extremely uncomfortable, Deputy May pauses, choosing his words carefully. "I want to help you Miss Riley, I really do. But I don't think the Sheriff would like that…he's a bit…stuck in his ways."

I certainly don't want to get Deputy May in trouble. I also know that I'm going to need help. As a civilian, I don't have access to any of the technical tools or labs that I could end up needing. While I do have contacts at my old department, I know they can't allow me into the investigation without a badge. All I can do is try.

"I understand. I'm not asking you to open an investigation or anything official but I would really love to have your help. I don't know the area or residents here yet…if I could just pick your brain sometimes, it would really be appreciated."

Ah, the easy smile again. Did I actually find an ally here or am I just pushing my luck?

"I'd be happy to help you as a friend, Miss Riley. Nothin' official."

Chapter Twelve: Riley Morgen

Now that I have Deputy May on my side, I figure I should call Detective Ares at Minwall Police Department. He won't be able to tell me everything he knows, but maybe I'll be able to prod some information that hasn't been released on the news. More importantly, he needs to know about the necklace. It could be nothing, but I wouldn't feel right if I didn't at least try. I head into my bedroom and pull *Of Mice and Men* from my bookshelf. The majority of the books on the shelf are real, but this one is not. I bought it from some tactical store booth at a National Night Out event one year in Minwall. Inside the book has been hallowed out as a small storage for important items. Basically, a mini safe without the ability to lock. When I bought it, I figured it wouldn't get much use for anything of value, but more for important sentimental things that I didn't want to risk losing. I open the book and rummage through the few items I find important enough to hide and pull on the gold chain holding the locket. Again, turning it in my hands, I look for anything I didn't notice before.

I'm convinced this locket is supposed to open but the stupid thing is stuck. I press my fingernail into the seam and again attempt to pry it open. Nothing. Sighing with a mix of frustration and sadness, I resign myself to the idea that maybe this thing just doesn't open. I grab my phone and scroll through my contacts looking for Detective Ares' number.

After a few rings a familiar voice fills my ear, "Morgen! You ready to come back or you still roasting marshmallows in the woods?"

Laughing, I reply, "Ares, we all know s'mores trump patrol any day."

"I can't argue with that logic."

"As much as I miss you guys, I'm actually calling about the Julia Preston case."

I can almost hear his demeanor shift just in his breathing. *Goodbye to my buddy, hello Detective Ares.* As he speaks, his tone proves his switch to professionalism, "Really? Do you know something about the case, Morgen?"

"Well, nothing concrete. See, I went out for a run here in Bearpoint and I found a necklace on the running path, it's called Binkin Trail. I picked it up thinking I would bring it to the local sheriff's department in case someone had reported it as lost property. After watching your last press conference about the Preston case, new photos of her were shown. In the photo of her wearing the green sundress, she is wearing a similar necklace. It could be nothing, but I just can't shake the feeling that it's too much of a coincidence."

I hear papers shuffling; I know Ares well enough to assume he is looking for the photo with the green dress. After a brief silence he says, "A gold, heart shaped locket?"

"Yes. I don't see any unique identifiers though. I've been trying to open it and see if there are any photos inside but it doesn't open. I'm not sure if it is stuck or the seam is just for show."

"Let me talk to Julia's family and see if there's any significance to this locket, or if they know she was wearing it recently. Hang on to that necklace until you hear back from me, okay?"

"Yeah, of course."

"I really appreciate you calling Morgen. Even if it's not related, it's good to know great cops still have their eyes open out there."

"Not a cop anymore, Ares."

"Once a cop, always a cop, Morgen."

Chapter Thirteen: Him

My last job has got me a little fucked in the head. Number 241 awoke the fire deep in my belly that took me years to master control of. Damn, I should have kept that one for myself. My mouth is practically salivating imagining that bitch begging for her life. The look in her eyes when she realizes no matter what she offers, there is nothing for her but death. The hot taste of her blood as it fills every crack in my skin. Now it's just wasted on that vile old man. But I'm not stupid. My needs have no place in my business. I will enjoy my own gazelle soon enough, but for now, another client needs his own.

The last five years have proven my business to be extremely successful. I give sick fucks the ability to enjoy the kill without the risk of the abduction. And let's face it. The abduction is an art all on its own. More killers get caught because of stupidity while grabbing a girl than the actual kill. Now-a-days there are cameras and witnesses everywhere, it's not as simple as being the strongest brute in the fight.

Some clients have higher standards than others. I personally don't give a fuck what their standards are, but my wallet fucking loves it. Whether it be a prostitute on the cheap or a young girl some family actually cares about, I know exactly how to deliver the product and get away with it. Like she vanished without a trace. I don't leave behind as much as a whisper of my presence. Once the product is delivered, I have nothing else to do with it. The girl belongs to the client.

The money belongs to me. This particular client has a taste for what he refers to as "classy girls". He must be pretty well off because he doesn't mind overpaying for the right product. Sometimes he's satisfied with a high-end escort type but sometimes he gets in the mood for an innocent. I mean, I get it. Innocents just react differently. And for sick fucks like me, that is everything.

With the last snatch so recent, I know it's a bit riskier looking for the same type again. Normally I would flat out refuse...or at least go to a different stomping ground. Like I said, this client can be very particular. And he's a good customer to keep happy. I don't want to lose this one...not when he's keeping my bank account ridiculously fat. So here I am. Back in this God forsaken city looking for more primo product. I bet he would have loved the last one. That asshole probably saw the news and knew my work. Let's be honest, I am the best.

Early in the morning is best for the higher end product. See, late at night prostitutes roam the street begging to get in your car and drunks stumble home without an ounce of judgment in those struggling brain cells...both make my job way too easy. Early mornings bring out the merchandise that actually give a fuck about themselves. At least enough to go out for a run alone or be rushing to some bullshit job they think is going to bring them wealth and happiness. Rushing along down the street worrying about what they can do to please their asshole boss today instead of noticing the man watching their every move. I admit these types are way more satisfying...I can understand why this is the preferred product to someone who does nothing but sit at home waiting for their delivery like I'm fucking Amazon.

So here I am. Five o'clock in the morning exercising my patience for the sake of artistry.

I've seen a few choice candidates already but it just isn't exactly what I'm looking for. There's plenty of reasons I'm so good at what I do, one of them being my natural ability to select the perfect victim. I take the time to choose the best of the best, and I always get what I want. I don't make mistakes and I don't bring the client disappointing product. Most importantly, I don't put myself at risk of being involved in any potential activity with the pigs. I know the streets and businesses without cameras, and I never do a job in the same car twice. I would never leave an obvious link between jobs, not that anyone will ever see me to give a description. I was literally born too smart for a stupid world.

A petite blond with huge fake tits walks down the sidewalk toward my vehicle. The sound of her high heels clicking against the concrete tickles my brain.

Click. Click. Click. Click.

Her skirt is nearly short enough to give anyone trailing her a show, but long enough to force men to stare, hoping for that momentary rise she'll pretend is accidental. I would say she's just some slut moonlighting as a street walker except the blazer she's wearing suggests she's on her way to work. The purse slung over her shoulder has some mix of the alphabet prominently displayed which I'm sure proves she's spent a few hundred dollars on it to other women who actually give a fuck about those things. She's on her way to work early to some job dominated by men who care more about her giving them something to look at then any actual value she could add to their business. She probably believes that one day they will see her as an equal instead of just a pretty face. People are

43

so predictable. There's that all knowing piece of my brain snapping into place.

She's the one.

I quietly get out of my car and slowly make my way onto the sidewalk. There are all different ways I could go about this. With a prostitute, I don't even have to try…just offer the skank a few bucks and she'll jump in the car like she's just begging to die. No fun in that. Sometimes with the better product I'll choose to offer them a ride, or an ear to listen, or just act interested sexually. The true artistry in the abduction isn't knowing the area. Sure, having no video evidence is important, pivotal even. But the true artistry is approaching a victim and in under a minute, being completely sure which approach will result in her being inside your vehicle riding to her death. The best result is going to come from an approach that involves zero screaming, zero awareness or suspicion. No one suspects an abduction is happening when a woman is willingly getting into a car. That type of thing doesn't stick in anyone's head…even when they see news bimbo's story a few days later. Considering the possibility of unseen eyes watching us both, I decide on the willing route. Less fun maybe, but necessary when doing another job so soon after the last.

Click. Click. Click. Click.

"Excuse me, Miss?" My voice careful to be smooth, not a hint of the adrenaline hidden beneath my veins. I smile casually as she turns to look behind, eyes meeting mine.

"Yes? Do I know you?" I can hear the slightest tone of fear in those words, although I am impressed that she has attempted to pretend she is unafraid of being summoned on city streets that offer only patches of light from the

44

streetlamps. As our eyes meet, I feel the change. She is interested…attracted to what she sees. *I have her.* Just like that, a moment passes between us, and I know how this will end for her. My blood begins to surge with excitement, but outwardly I maintain my casual visage.

"Unfortunately, I don't believe so, no." I smile appreciatively of the vision filling my eyes. The eyes and the smile…enough to have any gazelle's guard down. "I believe you dropped something." I bend and scoop the object into my fingers, then open my hand, willing her to see.

She looks confused for a moment, they always do, clutching her handbag and checking that the zippers are secure. "What is it?"

I extend my open hand toward her but remain glued to my spot on the sidewalk. *Let her come to me.* In my experience, I have learned that subtle gestures can make or break perceived trust quickly. I am a lion; the gazelle must come to me. Even walking towards her in this setting may feel threatening, and the last thing I want is to set off any warning bells in that peroxide-soaked brain.

She seems to consider it, that I may be a threat. Just some stranger on the street. But I know better than that…she will lean on two things. I am attractive. Not just enough to take home drunk one night at the bar…no. I am write home to your mother, dream of what beautiful babies we'd make, fantasize about me fucking you against the wall, attractive. Anyone with eyes knows it. And let's face it…attractive people can't be killers. Two, she is a gold digger. The type so obsessed with how she is perceived that she needed plastic surgery, expensive clothes and bags and she will be unwilling to disappoint an attractive man.

45

I remain; hand extended holding a white gold diamond tennis bracelet. The glint from the light has her attention, the curiosity is obvious. She walks towards me, closing the distance with the *click, click, click, click*. I remain still, unfazed, unthreatening. As she steps in front of me, I smell a strong burst of perfume. I couldn't tell you the type or if it's expensive because no man gives a shit about those things. I suppose it could have been pleasant, had she stopped about half a bottle sooner. She stares into my hand, examining the bracelet, probably deciding if she should just lie and say it's hers. Get herself a new bracelet to show off to everyone who doesn't give two shits if she lives or dies. I could snap her neck right here. One swift move and end this pathetic life. I could grab her and have her in my vehicle begging for her life in under a minute. I swear, the patience I have learned in this job impresses me. There was a time that I was very impulsive, though it's hard to imagine now. My first few years of urges came with sloppy mistakes and very little control. If I were anyone else, I would bet the pigs would have found me already. But this is my calling, this is what I was bred for…and no one does this better than me.

The prey reaches out a single manicured finger and gently glides it down the diamonds. *That's right little gazelle, no need to worry about this lion.* She tilts her head meekly up, eyes meeting mine before she speaks. "I wish it was but that's not mine. It sure is beautiful though."

"Keep it." I state simply, extending my hand toward hers.

"Oh, I couldn't do that. I'm sure some woman will be sick when she realizes it's missing. It's lovely and looks expensive." She looks surprised by the simplicity in my suggestion and despite her response, intrigued by the idea.

46

"You're right. Besides, this bracelet is for a woman who needs diamonds to enhance her beauty. You, I'm afraid, would outshine this hopeless little thing. It would be embarrassing for the diamonds, really." At this, she blushes. I have her entire attention now as she realizes that this handsome stranger is hitting on her. This is what she's been waiting for, praying for.

I smile and I can practically see her melting from the inside out. *Now that would be an interesting way to die.* She smiles back revealing a row of perfect overly whitened teeth. The kind of teeth she modeled after celebrities, thinking if I can't use them as headlights in the dark then they're too yellow. My client is going to love her. This is just his type. After a few moments of smiling like lovesick idiots in the street, I speak again.

"I know this is a weird way of meeting, but I feel like it's fate. God, that was probably so weird of me to say. Let me try this again. You're beautiful and I would like to get to know you better, do you think I could take you to dinner sometime?"

For whatever reason, women love when men stumble over themselves like idiots at the sight of them, at the chance of them. I've learned that it makes women think we're vulnerable. We're safe.

We're not going to drive you in our fancy cars to an awaiting psychopath to use you as a play toy before he watches the life drain out of your eyes.

As I knew it would, the flattery and perceived vulnerability have crawled their way under her flesh and keep her melting heart oozing. "That's not weird at all…it's actually sweet. I think it's fate too. I would love to go to dinner. By the way, my name is Meredith."

"Meredith." I repeat. "That was my grandmother's name."

No matter what the name is, I always say this line. Most of my work is unscripted, like an improv actor. But this line is always worth repeating when I am using this method of abduction. The whole fate thing is so fucking alluring apparently, and this just seals the deal.

"No way! It is totally fate!" Meredith practically squeals.

Now I know how thick I'm about to lay it on, but I'm about to get this chick in my car willingly. She needs to think we were put in this moment together to ride off into our happily ever after.

"The thing is…I'm named after my grandfather. It's like we were meant to be."

Chapter Fourteen: Riley Morgen

Waiting for Detective Ares to call with an update has been brutal. I would not call myself a patient person, and it's worse knowing Julia's life is probably in danger. I pace around the house, keeping constant check on the news for any new information. It has been two days since I spoke to Ares so I'm beginning to lose hope in the necklace being connected. It's probably just some runner's lost piece of jewelry. It could have dropped from the man in the green joggers I saw running ahead of me that day. Do men wear lockets? I didn't think so, but anything is possible. It probably has some family significance...or was a gift from a young love. I'm still glad I tried though.

Maybe this is just me obsessing over something that is completely unconnected. Maybe Ares is right...it's hard to turn off the cop brain once you become so used to questioning everything, looking for any possible connections. I can practically hear my mother's voice filled with worry and judgement now. *This is what you do Riley Rose. You can't let things go, and as much as I am glad you left law enforcement, you have to stop pretending you don't love this job.* I know my fictional mom is right, I do love this job. I love it for so many reasons, but I hate it for so many more. I wish I could explain to my mom exactly what this career has done to me. The things I have seen...the things I won't ever unsee.

The reality is, I know she couldn't understand, and I know that I wouldn't want her to understand. I wouldn't wish these memories on anyone. I used to believe that was a reason that I was meant to do this job, to protect others from the terrible truths of humanity. As so many of those terrible truths have built up in my head, I admit that no one, including myself, should be facing these things on a daily basis. Most people believe that cops are robotic, that these things don't affect us because of the way we are trained to be. Few humans are robotic enough to deal with hundreds of traumatic events a year, it is just unnatural. Each brick stacking higher and higher until eventually the weight of all those bricks becomes too heavy to carry.

Although the majority of any police department's employees understand this first hand, mental health has never been a priority in law enforcement. Instead, cops are taught that feeling these traumas, is weakness. I have felt these traumas…and I know I am not weak. The toxic culture I was immersed in only aided in a spiral that could have been prevented, had I been seen as human. Spiraling in the darkness of mental health struggles alone is the quickest way to drown. I refuse to drown in the waters clinging to the raft of a career. This is just one of the reasons I know that despite being born with an investigator's brain, I had to choose to swim to the raging river's edge and catch my breath on the bank. I don't know what I want to do with my life anymore, but I know that deep calling to help others still exists. I'm thankful that hasn't been taken from me. So, while I sit on this bank, breathing deep, I will give however much of myself I need to if it can help Julia Preston.

The familiar ringtone of my cell phone floats toward me, pulling me from my own mind. I race to my bedroom, ripping the charging cable from my phone and quickly answering after glancing at Detective Ares' name.

"Hey Ares! How's it going?"

A deep exhale fills my ear before he speaks, "Hey Morgen. I wish I could say it was going great but I won't sugar coat it. Sorry it took some time to get back to you; I've had a lot going on."

"I completely understand Ares; I'm sure the Preston case must be consuming all your time right now."

"It is, but it's only getting worse."

"Worse? I guess the necklace hasn't given you a new lead then."

"Actually, it's possible the necklace could be a lead. Julia's family said the necklace in the picture was given to her by her grandmother years ago. Her mother said she wore it a lot, but not necessarily every day. She's not sure if Julia was wearing the necklace when she disappeared. She is going through Julia's belongings in the apartment to see if she can find it there and will follow up with me as soon as possible. Julia's necklace does open, and has her initials engraved inside."

"Okay, well it still could be a possible lead, that's not a bad thing. Why is the investigation getting worse?"

Another deep exhale and I can imagine Detective Ares rubbing his face in exhaustion. The man has the same drive as me, there's just no giving up on a victim. "It hasn't been released to the public yet...but I trust you and I know it never hurts to have another good cop on the case. Morgen...another woman is missing from the city under similar circumstances. We believe they are related."

An immediate pit of anxiety burns deep in my stomach and threatens to swallow me whole. For a moment I convince myself I must have misheard Ares but the logical side of my brain takes over. "How long has she been missing?"

"She was reported missing after she didn't show up to work two days ago. That's what took me so long to call back. We got the report the morning after I spoke to you and I've been working nonstop looking for any evidence that the cases could be connected. I hoped it was just a young woman who left of her own accord, stayed at a new boyfriend's house or just got sick of the job and decided to quit. It's not looking that way, Morgen."

"Why would an abductor take two women from the same city in such a short time frame?"

"I've been asking myself the same thing. It seems way too risky for someone who isn't experienced in this kind of thing. Which has led me to the unfortunate truth that if this is related...it is really unlikely that these are the only two related cases. I've started going through old cases looking for any possible similarities but I just can't focus much of my time on sifting through old cases when the clock is ticking on two new cases. I'm requesting help, but you know how it is. Everyone is overloaded and it will take a few days before I can get enough people freed up."

"I wish I could help, Ares. You know I would if I was there."

"I appreciate that, Morgen. I can only ask for so much help from you since you turned in your badge, but you know I've always trusted your judgement."

"I'll keep trying to get the locket open. Let me know if you think of any other ways I can help."

Two days of waiting for some form of relief or answers from Detective Ares brought nothing but more worry and more questions. If his instinct is correct, I suspect this offender has abducted many more than two women. If that's true, what is happening to these women? Could this abductor be a serial killer? Is the offender a supplier for sex trafficking? Sex trafficking seems likely considering two women have been abducted within such a short period of time. Typically, with a serial killer, there would be more time between victims. Unless of course there was some major trigger in the offender's life that is causing a sudden change in MO. There are so many questions swirling in my head with very little information for me to go on. All I can do is speculate…and I hate stewing in speculation.

Accepting that I can't sit here driving myself crazy, I decide to get out of this cabin and go for a run. I leave my cabin, letting my feet choose the path as my mind is swirling with information. I walk down the dirt road that connects so much of the area around my new home. I absentmindedly glance around, noticing the other cabins in the area in more detail than I have before. The thick forest surrounding the area gives an illusion of being completely alone, although I have neighbors closer than it would appear from my property.

As I pass the neighboring cabin, I glance at the rickety porch railing and dilapidated front steps. My eye is drawn to sudden movement in the window, a figure holding back part of a blackout curtain and watching me walk by. Had I not seen the man watching me in the window, I would have believed the cabin was abandoned. If I were a different person, I would visit the cabin, introduce myself to my neighbors. I have no interest in that at the moment. I am peopled out for a while, especially with Detective Ares' conversation still fresh in my head. I need nature and sweat therapy, not some awkward introduction with a nosy neighbor.

As if my feet have a mind of their own, I find myself back on Binkin Trail running a steady but enjoyable pace. This place is truly beautiful. I mean, if you forget about the possibility of a missing girl's jewelry being tossed out like garbage in an area it is highly unlikely to be found. As summer is winding down, the air is becoming crisp in the loveliest way. The heat from the beating sun bringing a glisten to my skin while the cool air works to dry it before it glides down. Weather like this is my favorite time to go for a run. The solitude and sea of wooded green surrounding me is both soothing and terrifying. Not terrifying because I prefer company, but terrifying because my mind has nowhere to hide when I am alone. I tell myself I came to this town to face everything that consumes my mind but I worry that opening the gates will cause a flood so overwhelming that my gasping breaths will fill my lungs with the freezing rush of water.

I slow to a walk so I can fully enjoy the natural splendor engulfing my sight and force myself out of my own head. A few deep breaths of fresh air focus my thoughts on my body and bring my mind back to the present. As I open my eyes, I find myself slowly scanning the ground, subconsciously looking for any glittering glint peeking out from the grass. Bringing my thoughts back to the necklace, I decide I have to work on prying the locket apart soon. I'm so consumed in the idea; I don't notice the footsteps behind me until they are too close for my comfort. I whirl around, ready to defend myself and am met with a handsome smiling face that briefly weakens my knees.

"Hey there, Miss Riley!"

It takes me a moment to recognize him outside of uniform. "Deputy May, what are you doing here?" After the words leave my mouth, I realize it sounded a bit accusatory. Especially after noticing he is in workout clothes, most likely here for the same reason I am.

"Just out for a run, Miss Riley. I don't have work today and just couldn't stop thinking about what you said the other day. Figured I'd come out here and look around myself." If Deputy May noticed my tone, he gave me no hint of it in his response.

"Have you seen anything unusual?"

"Nothin' yet. Wanna help me look?"

I nod my response and begin a slow walk beside Deputy May. I've always considered myself somewhat tall, standing at five foot seven, but Deputy May dwarfs me. He must be around six foot four with broad shoulders that only add to his size. In uniform, I didn't notice the muscular bulges that now protrude from his tight t-shirt sleeves. With the way those cotton fibers are begging to be put out of their misery, I don't know how I missed it when we met. Many cops lose the energy to continue a consistent workout routine, and spent their days off completely burnt out. It's obvious Deputy May is not one of those cops. His caramel skin and dark hair provide an appealing contrast to his honey amber brown eyes. I admit he is easy to look at, not that I have any interest in subjecting anyone to my mess of a head. Still, it doesn't hurt to look.

"Where exactly did you find the necklace, Miss Riley?" Deputy May breaks the silence and brings me back to reality.

"It was about a quarter mile from here, just lying in the grass right off the trail. I'll take you to it."

Chapter Fifteen: Riley Morgen

Deputy May and I came up empty handed. Two hours of searching the area brought me nothing but a light sunburn and an appreciation for the deputy. At least Deputy May believes that this locket has got to mean something. Deep down, I know this could be nothing more than a wild goose chase, completely unrelated to Julia Preston, but I just can't let it go. I can practically hear my old partner from Minwall Police Department saying that's what makes me a good cop. Then my mother's voice jumps in and reminds me it also could be what drove me out of policing altogether. I admit that I get hyper focused on things, that I have a hard time letting go when I probably should. Especially now, I have no business being involved in a case when I am no longer a police officer.

I push my overthinking aside and know that I won't stop obsessing about this until it is solved. I can pretend it's just my feelings for Julia's family. My feelings for wanting justice and resolution for victims and their families. Selfishly, I also know that right now, I need this. I need a purpose other than fixing this fucked up head of mine. This is the cycle. This is exactly how police officers can bury more and more trauma and turn off any feelings that would be considered normal or appropriate to these situations. There is always going to be more victims, more cases and more situations to handle. There will always be Julia Prestons. The more I open my feelings or analyze what runs through my head, the less of me

I can give to bringing her home. Right now, this is my purpose.

I decide to head into town for some supplies at the hardware store. If I can get the locket open, then I will know for sure if this necklace is as important as my gut is telling me. I might as well get something to eat while I'm out too. Then I can work on the locket tonight and finally get the little gold heart out of my head for good. Luckily, in a place as small as Bearpoint, I can park my car in town and walk to every choice of destination the town offers. I park in front of The Conway and walk toward the hardware store. Walking inside is exactly as expected. A hodge podge of hundreds of items in a small storefront that smells like hay. The floor has a light coating of dust that I assume is from actual hay, or maybe just dirt brought in on patron's shoes. The smell makes my nose tickle and I rub it aggressively, hoping to stop any oncoming sneeze. The store itself appears to be quite clean, despite the floor, and rather well organized for such a random inventory of items. I guess when you are the only hardware store for at least forty miles, you end up needing pretty much everything in your inventory.

"Good afternoon, may I help you?" A store clerk comes from a back room, wiping his hands on a dusty apron and glancing toward me. He is strikingly good looking, and I stutter with recognition when I get the full view.

"Hey Jack, didn't expect to see you here too." I said playfully, trying to hide the surprise in my voice that I'm sure came across on my face. Does this man just work for every store in Bearpoint?

He chuckles and smiles, "No ma'am, my name is Brady. Jack is my brother. You must be new in town; I haven't had the pleasure of meeting you yet."

For a moment I am silent, mentally debating if Jack is messing with me or if he really has an identical twin. I don't know him well enough to be leaning either way, so I decide to just go with it. "I've been here a few weeks now; my name is Riley Morgen."

"Well welcome to Bearpoint, Riley, always glad to add some new faces to town. What can I help you find today?" His smile is warm and innocent enough that I decide he must be Jack's twin...or Jack is a really good actor.

Either way, I just want to get some tools and fill my aching stomach. "I'm trying to open a locket that is stuck. I need some small pilers, WD-40 and some kind of small tool that I can use to wedge it open."

Brady-Jack looks surprised for a brief moment, although he pulls himself together quickly. I wouldn't have noticed the slight shift had I not been vigilant at noticing people's expressions. Somehow his face seems harder before responding, "Sure, we have everything you will need here."

Brady-Jack motions for me to follow and starts collecting my requested items as we stroll down the overstuffed isles. As he turns to grab a small pair of pilers, I notice a scar just above his left jaw line. It is slightly pink and jagged; the skin raised from his otherwise perfectly chiseled face. I have never seen this scar on Jack's face before, and it is quite noticeable from the left side, I don't think I would have missed it.

He smiles warmly again and asks, "This isn't a common house project I hear about here but I suppose after wearing a locket for many years, I could imagine it getting stuck. How long have you been wearing it?"

His question surprises me. Why is this man so interested in my supposed locket? Or is he just making conversation? He certainly doesn't seem as smooth with small talk as his brother. My cop brain is telling me to withhold any information that isn't necessary, so I decide to lie.

"Oh, I've had it since I was a kid but it just sat in a jewelry box. When I moved recently, I found it and decided I wanted to see the photo of my Nana inside it again."

"That's sweet. Well, I really hope these tools help you do just that. Let me ring you up." While the words were sweet, his expression makes me uneasy.

Leaving the hardware store, I walk quickly toward The Conway hoping to prove if Jack-Brady is one man or two. If he's one, I don't know why Jack would play such a stupid joke on me, but I guess I hardly know the man. I know he's good looking, smooth talking, and works as a bartender. Or maybe a bartender and a hardware store clerk. Their personalities just seem too different to be one man, besides Brady had a scar. Does Jack have a scar that I somehow never noticed? I don't know why I'm so concerned with who Jack's sibling is or isn't, but the whole interaction just felt off...like he was hiding something. Great, another small detail to overanalyze until my own brain can't stand it anymore. *Oh, the joys of being an overthinker.*

A disappointing approach to The Conway's bar counter proved to be all the information I would get tonight. Jack isn't here. When I ask the employee who takes my order if Jack is working tonight, he states that he's off tonight, then gives me a look like I'm one of the many women hoping to hop on Jack, and I should cool the desperation. I order a burger with enough fries to drown myself and bring my mind back to the locket before heading home.

Chapter Sixteen: Him

Meredith the gold-digging skank is probably already dead. Sometimes I find myself curious how my clients kill. Not from a moral perspective, obviously, but just curiosity of the act itself. I want to be a fly on the wall, an observer or even better, a participant. I want to know every detail; I want to live it with them. I want to taste my victim's blood splattered in my teeth and hear them beg to remain in their shell of a life. I want to stare into the eyes filled with raw terror until the curtain is pulled and the fear remains frozen in time forever. Frozen in my memories…just for me.

I admit that baiting Meredith was fun, but it was no adrenaline rush. What is that asinine saying that people spew trying to give their pathetic lives meaning? *Do what you love and you'll never work a day in your life.* I'd love to tie each of the people living by that mantra up and torture them one by one before I find a unique way to part each of their souls from their bodies. Blood drenching every portion of my throbbing muscles while I smile and say *do what you love and you'll never work a day in your life.* If I'm honest with myself, I could spend the rest of my life doing just that and never getting caught. Just thinning the herd, a virtuous endeavor honestly. It's tempting at times, sure, but that would not pay the bills. Work for the bills, pleasure in my kills.

I've done this long enough to know when I am getting antsy. Nitpicking every little thing inside my head, frustration fuming at the smallest things. It's been building up since the old man's last girl and I need some release. What was it about that girl? On the outside she was no different than any of the others. Just flesh to be mutilated from bone. Blood to be spilled in a frenzy of joy and release. No...it was something inside of her, something ideal for a man like me. Some people are just so *killable*. Just so tantalizingly perfect for the roll of the victim. I would have savored every drop of her gore dancing down every ripple of my body. What I am so hung up on...so wrapped around...is that I think she would have loved every fucking second of it. Maybe even more than I would.

Chapter Seventeen: Riley Morgen

After returning home, I rush into my bedroom and retrieve the locket. Brimming with excitement, I lay out the tools I bought from the hardware store and examine the locket. First, I gently insert a small thin metal tool into the groove on the side of the necklace. The tool looks like something I would have found on a burglary suspect, possibly used to pick a lock. I assume it has an official name and use, but right now it might as well be named useless shit. Flipping the locket around in my hand, I examine the hinges. It's possible a hinge is stuck, preventing it from opening. It wouldn't have hinges if it wasn't designed to open, right? I gently dab WD-40 into the hinges and set it down on the table. Might as well let it sit for a few minutes.

I decided to be good earlier and had a soda with my burger instead of alcohol, but my nerves are getting to me now. It is so frustrating to feel so close to something, but have no answers. Nothing definite. This could all be nothing more than a snipe hunt. I pour myself a whiskey on the rocks and plunk down in front of the television. I'm not even going to kid myself by flipping through the channels, eventually ending up on the local news station. I dive in and go right to it. The small-town feel-good news stories should have a calming effect, but instead I just wonder why I haven't heard anything else on the Preston case. And why haven't I heard anything about the second missing woman Detective Ares told me about?

―――――― **** ――――――

I wake on the couch, the television humming in the background, and my mouth so dry it's nearly glued shut by dehydration. It must be the middle of the night; I should get in my bed. I sit up and rub my aching neck, regretting that whiskey that convinced me to close my eyes on the sofa. As I wobble across the joined living room and kitchen area, a glint from the kitchen table catches my eye. *The locket.* Immediately waking from my sleep induced trance, I rejoin my makeshift workstation, hoping the WD-40 has had enough time to work miracles. Lightly rubbing the hinges with one hand and grabbing the useless shit tool with the other, I gently restart the process of prying the little gold heart open. I have never enjoyed small intricate work, I feel like an ogre trying to thread a needle.

The sharp edge of the tiny tool enters the groove on the side of the locket, barely allowing myself to breathe, I give as much delicate force as I can, using the angle of the tool to my advantage. Slowly, I feel movement that I had not felt in my previous attempts. The crack in the groove is getting bigger… *it's actually working*. Once I am able to fit the tool inside of the locket groove fully, I reposition my hands and use my fingernails to do the prying. It was definitely the hinges…it feels like this thing hasn't been opened in decades. Feeling like a surgeon performing open heart surgery on the president, I keep every move precise, calculated, careful. Finally, I am pulling both sides of the locket apart and revealing the hallow insides that I have been obsessing over for weeks. It feels like the pieces could snap apart at any second. My eyes reach the left side of the inner heart first, nothing. No picture, no engraving. I quickly scan the right to reveal what my gut had been telling me all along…the small engraving of initials… 'JP'.

Chapter Eighteen: Julia Preston

I used to have a perfect life. I never thought it was perfect when it was mine though. I thought perfect meant there were never any problems, everything you worked hard for you achieved, and the invisible list of dreams we all have in our heads was filled with check marks. It isn't until everything is taken away from you that you realize how perfect you had it before. I thought losing it all meant losing someone you love, losing a good job or watching your life crumble after a painful divorce. I now know, that is the definition that perfect people use.

I try my best to hang on to myself here. I try to think about my family, but it is too painful to remember. The terror I feel in the darkness of this cage forces the memory of being a small child to pop into my head. I must have been five or six years old. I was terrified of the dark. Back then, the dark filled the comfort of my perfect bedroom, not a dog cage in a dirt pit underneath a monster's house. I sat in my bed, crying. Not a tantrum or loud sobbing tears seeking attention. Instead, it was meek, soft tears that burned heat against my cheeks as they rolled down thickly. Knees pressed against my chest, backed into the corner of my bed, the hard wall pressing into the flesh of my back. My mother entered the room wordlessly, seeming to understand my pain without me even sharing it. How could she have known? She strode immediately to me and sat on the bed, arms open, and I crawled to her. The smell of her hair filled my nostrils; the silk of her nightgown surrounded my legs. Words were never needed. She knew I needed her; I needed her comfort and her safety...and there she was. The dark was never scary when she was around. I wonder if she feels my need for safety right now. I pray she can't feel the pain inside of me here. It is easier to turn yourself off here, give in to the nothingness.

I am nothing here. The voice was right. I found out the voice has a name...Elaine. Elaine was abducted from the same city I was, but we would have never crossed paths in the normal world. I see now how sheltered I was before coming here...how little I knew. Elaine was a sex worker and addicted to drugs, which she says usually go hand in hand. I'm ashamed to admit that I would have never imagined how someone like Elaine could be a good person. But she is. She has become protective of me, almost like a big sister. I always wanted a big sister...and it is especially welcome in a place like this.

There are six girls inside this underground prison. We are all kept in dog sized cages that keep us bent, hunched on our knees for the majority of our existence. Hell, there are days when I considered myself lucky to have been chosen to leave my cage. If only to stretch my legs and unhunch my back. Every girl seems to be subjected to different things, though no one ever wants to talk about it. We all just stay hunched in our cages, detaching from our human selves and waiting for our souls to be forcefully extracted from our bodies. Except Elaine. I imagine Elaine's life before her abduction was already scary and maybe this isn't such a huge leap from what she was already enduring.

My captor is an old man who looks like he has lived an unforgiving life. The teeth still remaining in his mouth are rotten, and starving for company. I imagine he is around fifty-five or sixty years old, not frail, but weathered with his age. The type of aging that only comes from a hard life. The fact that he lets us see his face makes me think that no one will leave here alive. I haven't given up all hope yet, but I had to accept that hope means something different in a place like this. The first few days of my imprisonment, I planned my escape every waking minute of each day. I planned how I would overpower my jailor and run. Run from this unknown place and never stop. It was a good dream, a plot that kept my old definition of hope alive for a while. But the old man is not a novice jailor, it seems.

I am unsure of how many days I have been here. Most of my time is spent in a darkness so black, I cannot see my own appendages. It's probably for the better that I don't see what I look like now. For some time after I got here, I was never released from the cage. I was given no food, only a small amount of water once a day. I was sure I would die of starvation, or that my body had undoubtedly become deformed into the shape this cage has bent me into. At the advice of Elaine, I used my hand to dig a small hole in the ground under a corner of my cage. It occupied my mind for some time, and gave me a designated spot to call my bathroom…an ensuite, lucky me.

The old man keeps one light in this prison…somewhere in the corner of the room, away from the cages. There is only one time it comes on, and if it is shined on you, it is your time to go upstairs. I am often impressed with the stealth of his entry into this makeshift basement, but the wheels of the spotlight always give his location away. A slow drawn-out squeak that brings a vibration with its small drag in the dirt. It is amazing the way I can notice everything down here. The smallest vibration feels like an earthquake. The sound of a whisper, as if from a megaphone. By the time the old man had wheeled the spot light to my cage for the first time, I was too weak to be scared. I lay lifeless, assuming my burial was planned soon. The moment the light turned on; I felt a sensory rush I had never experienced in my life. It was incredibly painful, like both my eyes had ice picks driven straight through them and were skewering my brain. After hearing various clicks and metallic pings, the top of my cage lifted. My body lifeless, my eyes slowly moved overhead, staring blankly, seeing nothing but blinding light, wondering if my spirit was actually separating from my useless form of a body.

When you leave the cage, you are always shackled. Wrists and ankles bound, all connecting to a thick chain and box around my waist. It is fitting for the prisoners that we are. Unfortunately, it makes escape even more difficult than the starvation or injuries do. When I woke up in the cage that first day...I was terrified. I imagined everything you hear about from these houses of horror news stories...vicious rape coupled with a brutal finale to end the poor girl's controlled misery. I don't know what is happening to the other girls, except Elaine. The old man hasn't touched either of us like that...not sexually at least. Not once. No, he is reinventing the definition of torture for us.

I think he may be starving me for his own entertainment. Feeding me tiny bits, judging what is just enough to keep me alive, nothing more. I am given tiny morsels of food if he decides that I am being a good girl that day. I have never been so weak in my life. Probably another tactic to make sure I can never escape. Elaine tells me that I will get more food eventually…for now, I just have to focus on making the old man think I have broken. Broken for him, bent to his will and pliable to whatever he wants me for. She keeps telling me this is the only way to survive. I have to believe her…I want to survive.

Chapter Nineteen: Him

To master this art form is all about self-control. And to master self-control, means letting yourself off the leash every so often. I don't try to fool myself that these urges, these creative endeavors, need to be explored. Isn't the best part of a job well done, the little attaboy the boss so generously gives out? Well, I am a very generous boss, I must say, and my little reward awaits in the form of a whore who is ready to play. I know what you're thinking, how low, how pedestrian, for such a master of the craft. I would tend to agree, it is an easy target...a lazy target, perhaps. But truly, a smart target for a man like me. A higher value product is more likely to be missed, to have a family or at the very least a single person who gives a fuck about their existence. Product that spends every night wandering the street, begging strangers for money to get in their car, goes missing all the time and no one bats an eye. Even whore's families aren't worried when they go missing...they just assume they'll show up eventually or their body will be found OD'd behind some seedy motel. Society's degradation of street walkers has really made it easy on guys in my line of work.

Now here's where you see the true control. The heat is still on with that blond bimbo covering missing girl stories every damn night, so I relax. Take a little time off work, a little me time. A little time to stretch my legs and get creative...and who better to do that with than a waste of functioning organs like this tramp.

Even through the gag is shoved halfway down her throat, I can hear her whimpering. Like a wounded animal...so pathetic. I think when people imagine death, it's this dignified event where they go out like hero, or peacefully sleep and never wake again. Death is so rarely dignified...but don't worry, you won't be around to suffer the embarrassment.

"I'd like to experiment with some new techniques tonight." I smile, softly touching various tools and instruments on the table next to me. "I believe in keeping the relationship spicy, don't you?"

The whore's eyes widen. More whimpering, mumbling even. Maybe the stupid skank still thinks this is all some sex game and I'm just the kinkiest fuck she's going to have tonight.

"Good. I'm glad we're in agreement. Also, very important in a relationship, compromise...communication, man we are just covering all the basics here tonight. Really building a strong foundation, here. You know what... I'm proud of us." I almost make myself laugh with this one, I can imagine the whore's two brain cells in a full out brawl trying to get this one sorted out.

I have killed, or assisted in getting to that conclusion through abduction, 242 people to date...not to brag or anything. This skank is number 243. I have a very successful business, coupled with a healthy appetite. There's no way I'm not history's most prolific serial killer, not that I will ever get the true bragging rights I deserve. You don't get away with those kinds of numbers over fifteen years just to one day be caught. Always be in control. Always adapt. And in this case, always experiment.

"It is so important to try new things…never get stale. I am constantly trying to stay ahead of that uphill battle." I continue touching each tool, imagining what exactly each instrument could bring to my life…or take from hers.

My hunting ground may consist of mainly cities and over populated areas, but I will always be partial to the country. It's how I have lived my entire life. It's the way my ancestors for generations before me lived. It aligns with my core on so many levels really, and luckily provides benefits for those of us who choose specific artforms for a career path. I appreciate this fact silently as I stare at her hanging from a tripod game hoist with a gambrel in one of the barns on my property. There are only two differences between her and a deer. One, the deer would already be dead; there's no fun in prolonging an animal's death…that would just be cruel. Two, the whore isn't hanging upside down…I'm not a monster. Besides… I wouldn't want the blood rushing to her head and having her lose consciousness too quickly. I feel like that could taint this little experiment, and honestly, where's her fun in that?

I pick up a drop point knife, or as a country boy would call it, a skinner. I grab a stool since I will have quite a bit of work ahead of me tonight, no need to be on my feet the whole time. Standing in front of the strung up, gagged whore, skinning knife in hand, has gotten me practically giddy. The whimpering is in full force now, tears falling in rapid succession.

"This is why you are gagged. It's not because of a possibility that you could be heard. No…no one is around for more acreage than you can count. It is simply because I am not in the mood for a headache. I want to enjoy this; this is my vacation, and I have been working very hard lately. I don't

73

need to hear the screams, and begging to keep your sorry excuse of a life...I've heard it all before. And let's be honest with each other...this death will be more sensational than your life walking the streets looking for the next cock could ever be. Tonight, I just want to relax and unwind." I smile. This is met with sheer terror. I feel the familiar tingle of excitement on my skin. This. This is everything I needed.

"Now hold still 243, I want this hide to be perfectly intact. Or maybe I just want to see how much skin I can remove before you take your last breath. Oh, it's so fun to try new things."

Chapter Twenty: Riley Morgen

The discovery of Julia Preston's initials inside of the locket brought a new surge of attention to the case...and to the small town of Bearpoint. Police, as well as Julia's family, friends and strangers who were touched by the young woman's disappearance, have spent weeks organizing search parties and donating their time. Everyday ends with a sting of disappointment, no new leads, no further evidence. The family holds on to hope, and the police officers have started questioning if this is a search for a body. Each day that passes brings more likelihood to that conclusion. I get it, these types of cases don't often have a happy end...even when they do, the person that went missing is never the same person who comes home. For me, I am choosing to hold on to hope until there is evidence that I should not.

This alone feels like a step outside of the mindset of the uniform, and for that I am thankful. It is so easy to give in to what feels like logic...what the statistics tell us makes sense...choosing to hope, choosing to believe in what feels impossible, that takes courage.

Julia's mother chooses to speak at every search. She rallies these people together...family, friends, strangers. The strength of that woman radiates in this sole act. She will not give up hope. Her words still ring in my head, too powerful for anyone present to forget.

"My name is Audrey Preston; Julia Preston is my daughter. Julia is a bright and kind young woman who is just beginning her adult life. A life that is full of promise, and that is destined to change the world for the better. We cannot let someone else make the decision to take that from her, from us. Julia is still alive...of this, I have no doubt, and no explanation other than mother's instinct. I can feel her. She is still alive, but she is not safe. She needs us now."

A pause, everyone watching with bated breath, "By you showing up today, you have shown me that you too, are a kind human being who is destined to leave the world better than you found it. If it were someone else missing, Julia would be standing beside you right now, giving her time in hopes to help in any possible way. I thank you for being that person when Julia needs you most. Even the smallest thing can mean everything, as we know from her necklace being found in this area. Please, search slow and thorough. If you are unsure, or think anything seems off or suspicious at all, say something! We need that next clue now. A deepest thank you and show of our love from our family to each of you."

I asked Detective Ares not to inform Julia's family who I am, or that I had discovered the necklace. The hardest part of any incident I worked was the family showing up to the scene. That is something your brain can't disconnect from as a police officer.

Without any desire to, my memories force me back to my rookie year of policing. At this point, I had been out of the academy for less than two months...almost done with my field training. It was week seven on the streets and I had already been the log officer on six homicides. It somehow never phased me...it surged me with adrenaline and this deep desire to know who did this, to know why someone would do this to another human being. To find the truth through hard earned investigation and give the body lying at my feet the justice that any human being deserves. I never felt sadness; I never looked down and imagined the life that this person once lived. I didn't know that life…hell, most of the time, I didn't even have a name to give to that life until after the scene had been processed. Those circumstances make it easier to turn off an emotional response and rely only on logic. One shift during week 7 was filled with mostly traffic stops and answering unending questions from my field training officer about department policies and codes. It was about midnight when the tone came out for a shooting. The immediate adrenaline spike hit my system and I turned on my lights and sirens, speeding for a beat outside my own. A shooting in my precinct meant that the beat no longer mattered, it was all hands-on deck, so get your ass there and fill whatever roles need to be done. I arrived to two police vehicles and EMS already on scene and I ran toward the house, unsure of any details other than a woman had been shot. There was a young female, likely a few years younger than me, pacing in front of the house crying and screaming. Screaming at me I quickly realized, that her sister had been shot. I yelled to my training officer to stay with her and went inside the house. Two other officers were standing in the hallway, discussing theories and injuries. I passed them and saw a bedroom door, pieces missing, hanging from one hinge limply against the wall. A woman lying in the middle of the bedroom floor, a gunshot wound to her head, blood in a small pool around her. I watched as EMS worked on her. I stared into her open eyes and wondered if she could still hear me. I was still so young in this career and although the violence did not bother me, the idea of her suffering alone did. I bent down and set my hand on her arm, kneeling next to the EMT, showing more humanity than most officers had shown in some time, I imagine. At least I can be proud of that, I never failed to show humanity if I still could.

"Can you hear me?" I asked, still unsure if she even had a pulse, but knowing that I am not hurting anything by trying.

No response. But I suddenly realized the small movement of her chest, the small sign of life.

"Do you know who did this to you?" I tried again. A death declaration may be all I could hope for in this situation, but it would be a damning finale for the victim.

Her chest rose in a sudden, seemingly violent push and she let out a deep rattle, then stilled.

EMS informed me that was her final breath, giving me a time of death and began to clean up their equipment, repack their bags.

As I left the house to speak to her sister outside, I noticed the crime scene tape had already been put up, and an officer stood near the tape with a crime scene roster. Numerous police vehicles lined the area, and everyone had fallen into place. The roles had been filled and everyone worked like a well-oiled machine. This was the norm here. The violence, the shootings, the crime scenes. All completely normal...it becomes easy to forget that none of this is normal outside of this career.

The sister had been escorted to the other side of the crime scene tape and was speaking to a detective. An older woman and man were beside her, I assumed the parents had already shown up. Family members showing up to the crime scene is not unusual in this city, most of these citizens spend their whole lives here, raise their families here and are buried here beside their parents and grandparents. I used to wonder why, knowing how violent the last three decades had been here, why anyone would choose to stay and raise a family inside of this abnormal bubble. Realistically, I don't think everyone in this world has equal choices…and I can't judge them for that. We are all just doing the best we can. I walked towards the family, knowing that what may appear controlled now, has the ability to flip completely with just a few words. And it did.

At this point, we had the full story from the sister. Her and her boyfriend were arguing, as they often did, and it became ugly, as it often did. The difference this time was that her sister had been over the house visiting. Her sister defended her and took a punch from the boyfriend. Which I guess was not too much of a deterrent, because she struck back. I assume the boyfriend was not used to a woman who was willing to knock his teeth out. They fought and she ended up running into the bedroom and locked the door, screaming for her sister to call police. Her sister didn't call police until after her boyfriend broke down the door. After her boyfriend shot her sister in the head, at point blank range. After her boyfriend murdered her sister in cold blood. After her boyfriend turned to her and said "Bitch deserved it." then left the house. Domestic abuse feels so personal, but the reality is, no one around you can remain unscathed. And now her sister had given her life to protect her from her abuser. The man she loved took away what was the true love in her life.

When the detective gave the family the death notification, right then and there at the scene, I experienced the worst part of policing. It wasn't the crappy calls, the forced overtime, the regulars wasting your time with yet another petty call. It is the emotional aftershock that these crimes bring. The absolute ravaging of a family. I lunged for the mother as her knees gave out, and caught her in time to avoid her losing teeth to the pavement. I don't think she would have cared. I don't think she would have even noticed. She cried and screamed in my arms, screamed from a depth of pain I had never experienced before. Even though that was my first time meeting it, I could feel it like we were old friends. The pain was so deep, so heavy, so tangible, thickly filling the air around us... I could feel it in every pulse of my body. Every sob, every shriek, threatening to tear apart anyone within a mile vicinity. I felt broken for her and she was a stranger to me. I don't even know her name, but I know her pain intimately after that night.

I can imagine the pain that Julia Preston's family is feeling right now. The tiny strands of hope they spend every second tugging... so careful not to let them unwind, stretch them too thin, or tug them so forcefully the whole thing snaps. It is such a delicate dance, to hope.

I am outside of this investigation, thrown to it by chance, doing what anyone would do to support it. I do not wear the uniform anymore and the pain is not mine to carry anymore. I have enough of my own, and nowhere to set it down.

Two miles surrounding the area that Julia's necklace was found has been searched on foot. It may seem like a small area, but that took an impressive turn out of volunteers to cover so much dense forest and rough terrain. With nothing else found, the search area will expand but the volunteers will decline. It is a lot to ask strangers to hold on to hope that isn't theirs, to keep donating time that is already sparse for us all. There is no solid lead on a direction so the few people who will remain dedicated, will make extremely slow progress.

As I sit on my front porch, whiskey in hand, I can't help but feel frustrated. I have no other avenues to go down, no file of evidence, facts, or statements for me to comb through and find holes to follow up on. Just a fucking locket that I drove myself crazy thinking would be the key to finding Julia and it got us nowhere. Now it's just me and the millions of thoughts this case has stirred up, those years of artfully crafted avoidance had so carefully buried down. What am I supposed to do with all this anger? How is one human being supposed to absorb so many terrible things and remain unchanged?

This is why officers are trained to turn off this side of your brain, no good comes from digging up graves. In an effort to once again use my honed craft of avoidance, I begin to silently list the facts I know. The things about the case that I want to know. The things that I have the ability to find out. I know Julia Preston was here in Bearpoint at some point recently. Was it before her disappearance? Unlikely, according to her friends and family. She had been busy with working on some new work project lately and hadn't been outside of Minwall for some time. So, let's just say she was here after her disappearance. Would she have come here willingly, possibly running away from her life? Also, unlikely according to those who knew her well. While she loves the outdoors and spent a fair amount of time hiking, no one had ever heard her reference Bearpoint, there's no evidence that she had ever been here before. No one had ever heard of any new friends or boyfriends in her life, that could have ties here.

According to Detective Ares, none of her electronic devices had anything unusual. No searches of this area, no new contacts or conversations with strangers. Okay, so Julia came here after her disappearance, against her will. Is it possible that she dropped the necklace on purpose, hoping it would lead back to her? Sure, it's possible, especially if she did truly have hiking experience. Why choose to drop it there? Was it just an opportune moment when her captor wasn't watching or is there some meaning to that spot?

I need to talk to Deputy May. At least get some information about Binkin Trail and maybe try to find some connection.

Chapter Twenty-One: Riley Morgen

The street surrounding the sheriff's office is packed with cars. News trucks from at least seven different stations have crews standing around, surely discussing if there are any more stories to milk out of this town tonight or if they should just crawl back to the dregs of the city. People who certainly don't look like Bearpoint residents are walking the town's lone sidewalk, passing out fliers and asking locals if they have ever seen Julia Preston. I don't know that they had ever even seen Julia themselves.

I navigate around the clusters of people and enter the lobby of the sheriff's office. Thankfully, the lobby is completely empty...unfortunately it seems that includes a lack of any receptionist. I ding the bell on the desk a few times, enough to be heard without coming off as too annoying...hopefully. I glance up at the glass lining the reception desk and note a sign taped there stating "Sheriff Marks will not be making any public comment to the ongoing investigation into the disappearance of Julia Preston at this time. Please contact Minwall Police Department with any questions or requests for comment." I roll my eyes. Swift on going hands off I see...way to go Sheriff Prick, real hero we got here.

Ask and I shall receive apparently. "Hello Sheriff Marks, great to see you again." I smile what feels like the least genuine smile I have ever produced.

"You." Sheriff Marks doesn't even pretend to smile. "What the hell are you doing here? Come to stir up more trouble and worry my voters all over some silly girl who doesn't want to call home to her mama?"

The brashness of his statement takes me back. I came from a police department that purposely skews homicide numbers to make themselves look better and the chief would never make a comment like that to a citizen. I guess these country boys think they can do whatever they want without worrying about the politics and budgets. I bet this prick has been sheriff longer than I've been alive. "Great to hear the sheriff is so worried about the things that matter… like securing his votes, instead of you know, crime."

"Ain't no crime happen here girl. We're already cleanin' up the circus you brought here with your wild goose chase. Can't you learn to stay out of the way of the men actually doing this job?"

"Wild goose chase is a funny way of saying tangible evidence. And if I was looking at a man still capable of doing this job, I would gladly make room."

At this comment, Sheriff Marks' puffy face goes scarlet red. I have clearly struck a nerve, too easily, I might add.

"Get out of my building girl before I arrest you for trespassing…and consider yourself lucky if I let you stay in this town."

I consider letting every smart-ass comment run freely from my mouth, but instead turn and walk out cooly before I let my mouth get the better of me. I am not here to make enemies, especially with some half ass cop who's overstayed his position by about thirty years. Deputy May said the sheriff was stuck in his ways, but I didn't realize that included blatantly turning his cheek to a missing person case in the name of never losing a vote. Is it really better to pretend crime will never occur here than to face it head on relentlessly when it does? Politics mucks everything up. I'm going to have to figure out a different way to talk to Deputy May, because I get the feeling that was the last time I will be chancing a friendly visit at the sheriff's office.

Chapter Twenty-Two: Riley Morgen

The unfortunate side effect of not letting the venom spew from my mouth straight into Sheriff Prick's face, is that it now sits bubbling in my belly. I imagine molten lava dancing inside of my stomach, rolling and popping, laughing at the destruction they are destined to bring forth. Years in law enforcement has taught me the ability to pick my battles, to hold my tongue for the benefit of my job. It did not teach me what to do with that anger when it doesn't come out. For right now, there are two ways to deal with pent up emotions that can't be let out...drink or sweat.

I lace up my running sneakers and head out of my cabin door into the fresh air. I'm still angrily cursing the sheriff under my breath but the boiling feeling in my stomach is finally beginning to subside. I think if enough of those under the breath names come out, I will finally have put out the little fire. The sheriff being upset about bad publicity is understandable, especially in a small town where people believe they are safe. But the way he acted was so unprofessional, and honestly misguided. Why was he so upset that I happened to find the necklace and told Minwall Police about it? I tried to tell him first so that he wouldn't feel blindsided by the aftermath. Ugh, this is the worst thing about policing in today's world...the politics. Somehow perception has become more important than the truth. And that is a dangerous place to be.

As I pass by the dilapidated cabin that I have the displeasure of calling a neighbor, I again notice movement in the window. A male figure, pulling back a blackout curtain, stands front and center, watching me shamelessly like I'm some circus act. What does this old man want? Is there no shame in his surveillance of his own neighbors? I roll my eyes and angrily huff at his intrusion. I am sick of feeling like an outsider here. I am sick of being an outsider nearly everywhere. Ever since putting on a police uniform for the first time, I became an outsider everywhere but inside of a police department. I nearly turn and stomp up the ghost of a driveway, now covered in weeds and grass, just to pound on this man's door and ask him to pay admission to this freak show. I might as well start charging for it. I stop abruptly but force myself to continue past his house. This is not how I want to speak to a neighbor for the first time. Especially some elderly man who more than likely needs a neighbor to help him out with things he can't keep up with anymore. No, this anger is not his. This anger is for the sheriff alone.

I realize that without having any destination in mind, I am jogging towards Binkin Trail. Even my subconscious can't let this go.

Mentally updating my "I can't trust you" list, I add Sheriff Marks. I admit that he's probably just pissed at the bad publicity and only worried about his campaign, but it is possible that he doesn't want to highlight the connection here for other reasons. Either way, it's pretty despicable for the sheriff to try to sweep something like this under the rug. After the strange interaction I had at the hardware store, I might as well add Jack-Brady to the list too. I still don't know if that is one or two people being added to the list, but something

87

about the whole thing just feels off. I admit, probably not snatch a girl off, but it's just another thing for me to follow up on eventually.

Just as I finally start sweating out some of this anger, I hear a male voice shouting my name. I turn to discover Deputy May, in full uniform, jogging towards me.

"Hey May, what are you doing up here in uniform?"

"Miss Riley, I'm glad I found you. Sheriff Marks sent me up here to make sure all the reporters had cleared out. I don't know what you said to him, but he is pissed. I don't think you should plan on any social invites anytime soon, makin' an enemy out of him."

A chuckle escapes my throat, "I appreciate the heads-up May, but he deserved everything I said. I just hope I didn't get you in any trouble."

"None at all Miss Riley. Were you down there lookin' for me?"

"I was actually. I just wondered if you knew any history of Binkin Trail...or maybe how many houses can be accessed by the trail."

"I know it pisses off the sheriff, but I really appreciate how you think Miss Riley. You are a good cop."

"I'm not a cop anymore, May."

"Once a cop, always a cop, Miss Riley."

Chapter Twenty-Three: Riley Morgen

With Deputy May's promise to get me all the information he can, I come back home to find an unmarked envelope laying on my porch, in front of the door. Considering that mail isn't delivered to homes in Bearpoint, this strikes me as odd. The homes are widespread and, in some cases, far off the typical roadways so everyone receives their mail from PO boxes in town.

Instead of immediately checking the envelope's contents, I go back down the steps and check the surrounding area. Slowly, I walk my property looking for anything out of place. Especially for the possibility that someone is lying in wait for me. Satisfied that no evidence other than the envelope was left, I pull a tissue from my running shorts' pocket and pick up the envelope as I unlock my front door.

After putting on a proper pair of latex gloves, I sit at the kitchen table, gently opening the envelope. As much as I'd like to believe it is filled with nothing but a love letter, I have seen too many officers haphazardly open folded paper or envelopes, only to get a face full of unknown powder. Then you win the chance to spend a night in a hospital, seeing if you overdose and wondering what the hell has entered your lungs. Not a prize I'm interested in.

I pull a folded piece of paper from the envelope and gently unfold it, carefully holding my breath. There is no powder, no unknown substance. Just a typed letter, one sentence long.

"You are going down a road you cannot come back from. Stop looking before someone stops you."

The letter feels lightly threatening, and clearly, it's no longer a secret where the girl who found the necklace lives. Who would leave this for me? Deciding that being threatened is doing absolutely nothing to resolve the anger I still feel for Sheriff Marks, I grab my car keys and decide to make good use of my time and energy.

---- **** ----

Forty minutes later I am in my old stomping grounds, Minwall. The city is now in the cover of darkness, bringing me back to all the years of my life on night shift patrol. In the darkness of a violent unpredictable city, this city, I feel at home. I imagine that I am still wearing the Minwall Police Department uniform, the blue and white patch donning my upper arms. Where would I be canvassing right now? Where would surveillance make sense if I wanted to know more about Julia Preston's abduction?

I drive towards the nicer area of the city, the area that Julia Preston lived...the area she was taken. As I approach the block of her apartment building, I begin to look for cameras in the area. For such an expensive area, there is a real lack of city cameras. I guess they justify it by saying this is a low crime area when compared to the rest of the city. I wonder if any of these buildings have lobby cameras that may have seen Julia running by that morning, completely unaware of how everything was about to change.

I park in front of Julia's building and decide to go on foot. I want to take the exact route that she did. If there is anything small, anything unusual...I am way more likely to see it on foot than driving by. I walk slowly, scanning the ground and glancing around curiously. Two girls pass by me on the sidewalk, giggling and paying no attention at all to the world spinning around them. They are blocks from where a woman was abducted, and don't appear to notice anything going on around them. An easy victim to an unfound monster. I shake my head and keep walking.

Detective Ares said that there was no evidence of Julia ever making it to Lawson Park. Somewhere along this walk, someone grabbed her. I glance around, feeling the prickling of my skin, suddenly feeling like I too, am being watched. Preyed upon. In a city like this, how could no one have seen the abduction? Not a single person looking out of all of these windows surrounding the sidewalk? Or could that be the perfect place for someone to watch their prey? This man knows what he is doing and he knows the area. This is a seasoned professional...not a crime of opportunity, it was a plan that has been perfected by practice.

Throughout my walk, I am disappointed that I have not seen a single patrol car. Not surprised by any means, but disappointed at the lack of presence. In a city that has heinous crimes happen every day, officers' memories tend to be short and their time stretched tissue paper thin already. I don't blame the officers because I know the consequences of staffing problems in a police department. It still just feels unsettling.

I find myself walking into Lawson Park and using the flashlight on my phone to look around. It is such a small chance that I will find anything, all this time later, that police haven't found already. I admit that it feels good to be doing something, anything, that could be productive for this case. Even if it is likely nothing will come of it. As I search, I realize I have been in the park much longer than I intended. It is getting late and there is one more thing I want to do before going home.

I drive toward my old stomping grounds, my beat, the area I patrolled for so many years. I could be putting myself at risk here, walking the streets in a high crime area at this time of night but I have a plan. I pull into a parking lot near the Eevee Motel. A place known for drugs, prostitution, and violence. I know the motel well enough not to bring my car into the parking lot, a one way in, one way out death trap for someone who is not wanted there. I make sure I have nothing of value on me, quickly put on a hoodie I keep in my car, ensuring the print of the firearm on my hip is well hidden. I check my pocket for the folded paper, the latest missing flyer of Julia Preston. Exhaling a deep breath, I leave the car and walk down the streets of Minwall.

I see an escort walking towards me, glancing towards the road, paying me no attention thus far.

"Excuse me, miss?"

She looks at me, her eyes tired and heavily blackened by eyeliner. "Yeah?"

I pull the folded paper from my pocket and open it quickly, "Sorry to bother you. This girl was abducted from Minwall and I'm just wondering if you know anything or have seen anything strange?"

She takes the paper, looking me up and down suspiciously, then glancing at the picture of Julia Preston. "I don't know anything." She hands me back the flyer.

"Have you seen anything strange around here lately? Like a car or person that doesn't belong?"

"What are you, a cop?" Her hand is on her hip, staring me down with a disgusted look on her face.

"No, I'm not a cop. I'm just worried about her."

"She's a pretty white girl. The cops will actually look for her. She'll be fine." She turns and begins to walk away from me, clearly done with our conversation, but I am not.

"But what if she's not?"

She stops and turns to face me again. "And what about all of the girls out here walking the streets every day that get taken? None of them will be okay, and none of you will care. According to y'all, we were asking for it. Shouldn't have been out here selling ourselves for drugs. Like we don't have families to feed."

"I care. Are there girls you know out here being abducted?"

"Abducted. Raped. Beaten. Killed. It happens to us all the time, the fact that you don't know that just proves my point."

I shake the flyer in the air as I speak, "And maybe some of those cases are connected to this girl too. If you don't tell anyone, then how can anyone help?"

"How are you going to help? Walk the streets with our picture too?" She chuckles sarcastically.

"I would do whatever I could for any woman. Did one of your friends get abducted within the last month or so? Please. I'm just asking for information."

"I didn't see nothing. But I heard one of the girls who lives in Eevee got picked up by a John and never came back. I don't even know her."

"Do you know her name?"

"Nope."

"Did they give any description of the man or the car?"

"Just said the John was good looking… and young."

——————— **** ———————

As I drive back home to Bearpoint, a million thoughts swirl through my mind leaving me feeling restless. Who could have left me that note? And is this young- and good-looking man in Minwall the person who could have taken Julia Preston?

Chapter Twenty-Four: Julia Preston

Today is my turn to go upstairs. I have no idea how long I have been away from my home. I feel an immediate pang in my chest at the thought of the word. Home. The word used to bring so much hope…gave me so many memories to hold on to. Now it's just pain. Hope is too dangerous in a place like this. I'm starting to wonder if this is my new home now.

One of the other caged girls had her day upstairs last week. When the old man came to get her, everything felt different…but the same. The old man's breathing sounded different…more labored, more hurried. His steps more prominent, less stealth to his movements. The method was the same. Elaine said I'm losing it down here, noticing things like that asshole's breathing. I don't know how she doesn't notice, when that is the only human interaction we get besides whispered conversations in the solid blackness to each other. The girl never came back downstairs. I could hear her screams for hours that day, when the silence finally came, it was even more disturbing than the screams.

Everything was different and the same. I realized that night that I never knew the girl's name. I had never heard her speak anything other than the word "no", which she chanted endlessly every time the old man was near her. I felt a deep pang in my chest for a nameless girl that I had never known, yet had known better than I even understood. The pang had nothing to do with hope. Elaine says the girl didn't break. The faster you break, the longer you live, according to Elaine. No one knows how long they have been down here, but Elaine seems to have watched so many girls come and go. She seems to understand this place.

"Whether it's real or fake, the faster you break, the less it will hurt." I can hear Elaine's whispered words replay in my head.

I am chained and shackled to a chair in the upstairs. As my eyes are finally adjusting to normal light, I can see the old man getting his tray ready. He always prepares a tray before sitting next to me. The tray contents are different every time, but its presence is guaranteed. We are in a shabby kitchen that appears in desperate need of repair. The few cabinets that remain seem to be rickety, doors swinging limply from the rusty hinges. I see a window above the kitchen sink, but no light comes through it. At first, I thought that I must come upstairs only at night. Now I believe that no light ever comes through that window. Maybe it is boarded up...maybe it is just for show. I never know what is real here anymore.

The old man sits in front of me and studies me before writing in his notebook. He does this every time. I feel like an exhibit at the zoo, or the subject in a scientific experiment, but I have learned to remain silent. I am only to respond, never to begin conversation. He then sets down the notebook and moves the tray beside him. I can see small objects on the tray, some type of food maybe.

"How do you feel, Julia?" His voice makes me jump, although I should have been expecting it.

I know this game, I know he does not want to hear how I truly feel or what I think. I have learned that the hard way. He says I am lucky he believes in a breaking in period.

Elaine's words race through my head constantly...*the faster I break, the easier it is...the faster I break, the longer I live*...or at least the better actor I become, the easier it is. Sometimes I worry that my acting skills are only tricking myself...maybe I am breaking for real and holding on to some false hope that I'm still me buried deep, deep down.

I take a steady breath, willing myself to show no fear, no upset to my voice or face. "I am thankful to be upstairs with you today."

He reaches for a small item off of the tray and presses his fingers to my mouth. I open obediently and he slides the small, smooth praise inside. My mouth bursts into an immediate flood of chocolate and creamy peanut butter. The sensation brings tears to my eyes. A buckeye is a candy that will always make me remember my grandmother, but it has never tasted as good as it does when you are being fed only just enough to keep you alive.

"I can tell you like that, Julia. I want to keep giving them to you, but I also want you to be a good girl. When you are good, then I am happy. When I am happy, I want to shower you with love and treats. Do you understand?"

"Yes, I understand. Thank you."

"Such a good girl today." He smiles; those rotten teeth giving the illusion of a black hole, he strokes my hair and places another candy in my mouth.

I would be completely grossed out, if I wasn't so thankful that today is a good day.

A happy day.

Chapter Twenty-Five: Riley Morgen

Who would have left me a note like this? I'm not sure if it is taunting me to play some sick game with them or warning me that I shouldn't be playing the game at all. The most concerning thing is that whoever has some involvement in this game knows where I live...and knew when I was out of the house. A sudden chill runs down my spine as I get the sensation of being watched. I glance around again, my eyes finding nothing but a vast expanse of greenery and a sudden awareness of just how alone I am in this cabin. I have never feared people, or even feared the heinous acts they can commit against each other. But since I have left law enforcement, I feel stripped of some piece of me. Some armor that was not tangible, but came from facing death head on every day. I am left with a gaping emptiness that seems to fill only with a pool of anxiety...and uncertainty. I don't fear what this person could do to me, involving me in this game. I certainly don't like the idea of being prey, though. I have to get ahead of their next move. That's what a game of strategy is all about...being one step ahead.

It's hard to know someone's next move if you can't even pinpoint who that person is. This note could have been a warning from Sheriff Marks. It's possible he is just trying to scare me off, get me to stop so that Julia's story becomes old news fast. Could the note have been left by whoever abducted her? If that was the case, I must be getting closer to something that has them panicked. But if that were true, that means the abductor…possibly killer…knows who I am. I haven't been in any news broadcasts or openly active in this investigation from an outsider's standpoint…which would mean that whoever did this is someone already a part of the investigation, or that knows me personally. It wouldn't be unheard of for the guilty party to help out with the search parties or want to know more about the inside information of the investigation. There have been so many people coming into town to assist, it could be any number of people I've never seen before. But they must have seen me to know that I'm involved…and to figure out where I live. I've got to create a suspect pool so I can start getting ahead of this.

I grab a brand-new notebook out of the small stack I keep tucked away in my bedroom closet and head back to my kitchen table. I have always been a list maker. There's something about seeing everything written out in front of you that brings some clarity to my constantly full mind. I start by making a list of all the knowns of the investigation.

Julia Preston, 21, last seen leaving her apartment in Minwall

Known to run in Lawson Park on the west end of the city, it is believed this was her destination the day she went missing; never arrived

Unlikely that she left of her own accord; young professional; strong family ties; no signs or history of mental health struggles

Julia's locket found about 40 miles outside of the city, in Bearpoint

Julia has no known ties to Bearpoint

It's a little depressing feeling so close to this investigation, but being so far away in reality. Without being involved in the actual police investigation, I know this list can only be so long. I don't have the insider information that an officer working for Minwall Police Department would have. I honestly feel pretty thankful that I've gathered what I have on this list, just from conversations with Detective Ares and gathering whatever information I can during search parties or news stories.

I flip the page to a clean slate and title this list "Need to Eliminate, Possible Suspects:". This will have to be the running list of people I need to look into. I don't have any true suspects yet. I guess if I had enough to think I had a suspect, then Detective Ares would have had enough to be getting warrants on the guy already.

Sheriff Marks – find out why he is such a prick...hiding something? Or just born that way?

 Brady-Jack / Jack-Brady – really twins or some childish small-town boredom prank? Does Jack have a scar on the left side of his face, above his jaw line?

Runner guy – he was near the scene when I discovered the locket; identify him

Deputy May – on my side or wants to be close to the investigation for information?

The list is depressingly short...and really just a question of why the people of this town seems to be a bunch of abnormal weirdos. Of course, there's a huge possibility that the offender isn't even on this list, so I will have to remain alert and update with anyone that seems suspicious. In the meantime, at least I can focus on proving who on this list can be trusted.

That note was either supposed to scare me off or challenge me to a game. Whoever it is…they better get ready…they've never had an opponent like me.

Chapter Twenty-Six: Him

Number 243 was quite a bit of fun. I love learning new things…like how much skin I can peel from a whore before she loses consciousness. I give it to her; she did better than I expected. I wonder if she was high or just used to being treated like an animal. I learned that if you are a master of a knife, like I have become after so much practice, then you can skin an entire human without nicking any arteries or organs. I learned that the shock a body goes through will make you lose consciousness before anything else…but definitely not in a timeframe that benefits the skinless.

Years of mastering my craft has taught me to never lose control. The best way to keep control of your own appetite is to let yourself off the leash every once and a while. It's like taking an all-expense paid vacation after winning the employee of the year award. I always win the employee of the year award in my company. No matter that I am the only employee. Now that I have had my relaxing reset of a vacation, I am ready to get back to work with a clear head. Urges controlled.

It has been a few weeks since my last job, and while each grab pays well enough to ensure I can lay low for a while afterwards, I do get bored. Pretending to live a normal life is in no way entertaining enough for someone like me. Someone special. The mirage of a normal life is one of the reasons it is so easy to stay off the radar, I don't pretend to be regular for the enjoyment of a typical job and mundane existence. You think serial killers can just run around beheading every dumb fuck that pisses them off and avoid detection forever? It is all about blending in with the herd without anyone ever noticing that you are indeed the wolf.

"I'm telling you the whole thing is too close for comfort." I am snapped back from the pleasantries of my mind to the grating nagging of my brother's voice.

"And I'm telling you that I have nothing to do with it. I gave up on those urges long ago. If someone in Bearpoint happens to snatch a girl and get away with it, then more power to them, but it wasn't me. Don't you think you would notice if that girl on the news was here? We live together for fucks sake."

"Did you kill her?"

"I did not kill her. I'm your brother, you know me well enough to know if I was lying. Can you just drop it already?"

"That's why I can't drop it."

He does not know me well enough to know if I am lying, clearly. I did not kill that girl on the news, I killed some other girl that the news will never give two fucks about. That's the beauty of a prostitute…they're the world's freebies.

I've always known doing business with the old man is risky, considering we live in the same town and both have roots to the people here. I admit that as a kid, I hated that man. He has always been an arrogant asshole, so I was never surprised he was such good friends with my father. Unfortunately, I became indebted to him in the earlier days of my business. It has been long enough now that we have an understanding, each stepping aside to allow the other to attend to business unbothered.

"They say that cop who bought the Jenkins place found the girl's necklace on Binkin Trail."

"Good for that cop. Maybe she'll get some bullshit community hero award."

I, in fact, had heard about that cop finding the necklace, of course. In a town like Bearpoint, everyone hears everything. Even more impressive that no one but the old man has any idea about me. And fortunately for me, the old man is so wrapped up in it, that I have never once worried about him running that meth mouth around town.

"You're not worried about that?"

"Not even a little."

Chapter Twenty-Seven: Riley Morgen

I am running through a thicket of trees. Not running in an enjoyable way, but instead with a surge of adrenaline so thick and heavy, it feels like I am in a fight for my own life. I am drenched in sweat and feel the sting of salt in my eyes. I can see a figure ahead of me, wearing a dark colored t-shirt and green joggers, the man I saw near Julia's locket. I can't make out his features. A sudden pain in my right hand causes me to unclench my balled fist, revealing the gold locket. As I am getting closer and closer to the figure, he turns, suddenly aware of my presence. I feel my heart jump to my waistline as I see the blank face. Not emotionless, but featureless. It is as if he is wearing a mask of skin, or that he never had any features at all. No eyes, but seeing everything. No nose, but smelling the damp of the forest and fear in my sweat.

The trees suddenly clear and I am running through an open field. I can see concrete nearing my feet, inching closer with every pound of my foot. It feels like I am reaching a destination that I hoped to never reach. Suddenly I realize I am in uniform again, the locket gone, my duty weapon replacing it in my right hand. As I reach the concrete, I look up to see a boy...no more than fifteen years old, arm outstretched, pointing a gun. The gun isn't pointed at me...it's pointed at another kid. The second kid looks so small...he can't be more than twelve years old. I have never wished more that the gun would have just been pointed at me...please, not the kid. Please don't hurt a kid. I see my right hand raised, faintly hear my own screaming inside my crowded head. Please don't hurt a kid. He can't hurt a kid. I can't hurt a kid. I suddenly hear a gunshot, loud and clear, ringing in my ears, drowning out my own screams, my own pleading.

I wake on the floor of my bedroom, barely recognizing my own scream. My throat is hoarse enough to make me think I have been at it for a while. The nightmares are becoming all jumbled together, mixing my past and present into one giant pot of fucked up stew. How delicious.

After starting the coffee maker, I jump in a cold shower to wash the sweat and memories off of me. I know this isn't healthy. I know this isn't normal. Sleep used to feel like a break from the anxiety, from the constant hypervigilant state I had to live in. Now I can't even find escape there. I thought getting away from the city, away from this career would allow me to have a break from these feelings. Instead, it's like the dam has finally broken and a flood is rushing into every crack and crevice, filling my insides inch by inch with no route of escape. I'm worried I have no purpose outside of this career. Have I lost myself completely outside of being a cop?

After filling up my biggest coffee mug and turning on the news, I hear a knock at my door that nearly makes me drop the scaling hot liquid. You would think I wouldn't let a little thing like a visitor make me so uneasy, but it feels way more unexpected to have someone just drop by when you live in a town with a higher population of bears than humans. Peering out the front window, I lock eyes with Deputy May and see the smile creep onto his lips. I suddenly appreciate just how handsome he truly is and realize I don't really know much about May's personal life. I have noticed that his left ring finger is bare, and wonder if there is a girlfriend in the picture. I know I shouldn't even let my mind wander down this path after waking up screaming on the floor like I'm in some bad low budget horror movie from the 80's. I can't even imagine trying to explain that scenario to someone staying the night. *Oh, don't mind me, just testing out the acoustics in my new cabin...really is the ideal place for murderous screaming.* No freak show to see here, all completely normal. I snap out of my daydreaming as Deputy May starts waving a manilla folder in his hand, still smiling.

"Hey May, what you got there?" I say, pointing to the manilla folder still swaying in his hand.

Deputy May glances around, met by nothing but wilderness, and says, "Hey there Miss Riley, mind if I come inside?"

I am instantly intrigued by the desire for secrecy, even while remembering that his boss probably hates my guts and expects his employees to stay far away from me as well. I step aside to allow May inside and lock the door behind him for good measure.

"Why the sneaking around?"

"I just don't want Sheriff Marks gettin' the wrong idea about me being here. Much as he tries, he can't tell me who to be friends with...but he can tell me not to stick my nose in another department's investigation. I want to help you Miss Riley, I really do, but I can't risk my job over it."

"I wouldn't expect you to. If any of this is walking that line, you don't have to help me, May."

"I haven't hit my line yet, Miss Riley." He hands me the manilla folder and continues, "I got all the documentation I could from the library and the county clerk's office. There's some history on the area of Binkin Trail and a print out of all the current properties in that area."

"Wow! That's incredible, thank you so much. I think this will get the ball rolling on my investigation."

"Investigation? You be careful, Miss Riley. With the Sheriff as an enemy, you have plenty of eyes watching you now. I am helping you, as a friend just wanting to get to know your new town's history, just remember that I don't know anything about any investigation."

"I know. I promise you won't have any backlash from this." Even with May's warning, I don't feel the slightest bit intimated by the Sheriff and his goonies.

Our conversation is interrupted by a high pitched, urgent sound sequence indicating breaking news on the local news station. I walk to the couch and take a seat, steadying my breathing for the possibility of something terrible. Deputy May sits beside me so close I can feel the heat radiating off of his thigh. The blond newscaster appears on screen, face set in an almost stern visage.

"Breaking news out of Minwall this afternoon, as the body of a young woman found yesterday morning has been identified."

A small gasp leaves my lips and I see Deputy May's head turn towards me slightly. I didn't watch the news yesterday; I was so wrapped up in the note on my doorstep and making my lists for the investigation. Did they find Julia? Is she dead?

"The body of missing twenty-four-year-old woman, Meredith Stokes, was found on the side of route 60 yesterday morning when a passerby called police stating that they believed they may have seen a mannequin in a ditch and wanted police to verify it wasn't a person in need of help.

Meredith had been reported missing after not showing up for work and missing her niece's dance recital several weeks ago. We are live with Minwall Police Department for the press release providing more information."

The screen switches from the news desk to a small room filled with reporters standing around, mics held out, cameramen clawing for the best spot in the room. One podium stands at the front, the Minwall Police Department patch graphic etched into the wood. Detective Ares stands behind the podium, looking like he has chosen work over sleep lately. His short reddish blond hair neat, not a strand out of place, his white dress shirt crisp, tucked into his dark blue slacks so perfectly I question if he is wearing shirt stays. Ares is very good at appearing well put together, even when the pale purple circles under his eyes give him away. The small lines near his eyes more prominent with his exhaustion. I feel for the guy. Law enforcement as a career choice means accepting that you will be tired most of the time until retirement.

Detective Ares' mouth is already in motion while the news station completes the adjustment to the video and audio feed. Seconds, that feel like minutes, later I hear him speaking. We appear to have joined the broadcast at the point that reporters are asking questions.

"...For that reason, I am unable to provide any further information relating to that question. This is still an open investigation. Next question, please."

"Detective, do you believe Meredith's murder is somehow related to the Julia Preston case?"

"We are not ruling out that possibility. There are similarities, but not enough to say that they are undoubtedly connected. Although it has been over two months since Julia Preston's disappearance, we are still hopeful that she will be found alive. We have no evidence telling us otherwise at this point. For the remainder of the questioning today, let's focus on the case of Meredith Stokes. While the cause of death has not been officially determined by the medical examiner yet, we expect to get those results within the next few days. Even though we are officially awaiting those results, we are treating this as a homicide investigation at this point."

"Detective, were there obvious injuries that lead you to call this a homicide investigation prior to the medical examiner's official report?"

"Out of respect for the victim and the Stokes' family, we will not be releasing any details on the condition of Meredith's body at this time. I believe my statement that the investigation has now changed to a homicide is answer enough to that question without the need for any further details."

Even without being employed by Minwall Police Department anymore, I still feel a sense of pride whenever I see Detective Ares in his element. He always remains so respectful and professional...truly too good for such a shit hole department. The last time we spoke, Ares indicated that the Meredith and Julia cases were most likely related. I feel nauseous at the realization that if they are...what are the chances that Julia is still alive if Meredith isn't?

Chapter Twenty-Eight: Julia Preston

I'm convinced that your body can get used to anything. I'm not sure how long I have been in this cage, but it is beginning to feel like my normal. I feel sick at the realization of that. My body has accepted that I spend most of my time on my knees, back hunched, eyes to the floor. I barely feel the physical pain of my new existence anymore. I don't know if I could do this without Elaine though, she feels like all I have in this world. Sometimes I think about the old man as my family now too, and my heart aches at the word. Family. How can this man, the man who holds the key to my cage, be my family? I think he may be all I have for the rest of my existence. That doesn't even make me sad anymore.

I think about my real family a lot. I know they must miss me too…but it's been so long that I worry they won't find me. I don't know how long the old man will keep me alive. Girls go to the upstairs, then never come back. New girls will fill the cages eventually, Elaine says. I have cried to Elaine, wondering when I will go upstairs and never come back to my cage. Elaine says it's not going to happen to me…I think she is trying to give me hope. Such a small thing to hope for…remaining alive just to be a caged animal.

I know it could be so much worse. The old man isn't so bad to me or Elaine…I think she was right, if I let him think I have broken, then he will be good to me. I wonder if I am really broken, or just pretending. It can be dangerous to be too good at pretending…it can become your reality without anyone

111

noticing, not even you. I wonder how long it took Elaine to realize what she needed to do to protect herself, to stay alive. Maybe that's something she learned long before coming here.

Something about the darkness, never seeing the owner of the voice responding to you, makes being so raw and honest easier. Or maybe it is the knowledge that no one living in this darkness will make it out of here alive. Our whispered conversations have filled hours of darkness, the quiet voices seemingly so loud to my near dead senses. Elaine grew up in Minwall and had never left the city...until being abducted. Her life has been so rough, so much harder than anything I have ever known. For the little time that she actually had any family members, they showed her nothing but abuse and heartbreak. She was still a kid when she started working the streets of Minwall, first needing money just to eat and survive...eventually needing money for a drug habit she picked up. It's like she was never actually given the chance for a life...never even shown love. My heart breaks at that fact. If we never make it out of here, the best thing I can do is make Elaine feel love while we still have time. She deserves that.

"Elaine?" I whisper into the darkness.

"I'm here." She replies, as if I thought she may have dug an escape tunnel in the darkness without me hearing a single thing. I think she says things like that to be reassuring. Like without my sight, I might forget that I am not alone.

"How did it go earlier?" Elaine had been in the upstairs earlier today, and unusually quiet since returning to her cage. I hoped he hadn't hurt her upstairs, but I couldn't be sure in the darkness. I wasn't even sure what Elaine looked like...but I could tell her voice from a crowd, as if I had known her my whole life. Her voice had become a bright light in a world of shadow. I could tell her breathing from the other caged girls. Always so even and steady, so comforting those first few weeks when I was consumed by fear.

"It was a good day. He fed me a cheeseburger."

"A cheeseburger?" My mouth instantly waters. The idea of a cheeseburger seems so distant, so disconnected from my life here in this cage. "It feels like he has given me only a handful of food since coming here. Mostly crackers and candy. I'm barely more than a skeleton."

"But he is feeding you. That's more than some can say. You're doin' what you gotta do. Unlike some of the girls who come through here. When he trusts you, you will start eating good."

"I really hope so, I don't know how long I can last on scraps of food."

"You'd be surprised."

I inwardly cringe at Elaine's statement, wondering exactly how long she had to be kept alive with minimum food before the old man started feeding her again. Maybe starvation is something she knew long before living in a cage.

"Do you think we will be here forever? Will I spend the rest of my days in this cage praying I get to taste a cheeseburger again one day?"

"Jules, I don't know how long I've been here...years maybe? At least you have family looking for you. Just keep doin' what you gotta do to survive. Until we get out, we got each other."

"You don't need family to look for you. Your family is right here...in this damned cage, next to you. We will get out of this together." I said it as if it was a promise, and it felt like it was.

I want it to be a promise. I don't know if either of us will ever get out of here alive...but I know that Elaine is my family now.

Chapter Twenty-Nine: Riley Morgen

With the discovery of Meredith's body, the pressure I feel to find Julia has become even heavier than before. Detective Ares believes the two cases are related, and from the limited insight into the cases that I have, I wholeheartedly believe they are.

Deputy May left shortly after the Minwall Police Department finished their press briefing, and I have been combing through the folder of papers he gave me ever since. Apparently, Binkin Trail has a long history, and had been used as the sole road leading into the Appalachian Mountain range for at least a century before Bearpoint was even founded. As the town became more populated, at least more than just bears and deer, new roadways were established and Binkin Trail became a path primarily used on foot, or by ATV. According to the current map of the area Deputy May provided me, there are twelve properties that border Binkin Trail. The properties are sandwiched between a roadway and Binkin Trail, meaning that it is unlikely that anyone uses Binkin Trail to access their homes anymore. That also means that if I use Binkin Trail, I would be accessing the back side of these twelve properties, which may be a tactical advantage for me.

The map provided by the county clerk's office shows the property lines for each of the twelve plots, along with the names of the property owners. Unfortunately, I don't know many people in this area yet so most of these names will mean nothing to me. I scan the map, silently voicing the names to myself...Henry Michaels, Keegan Goode, Sean Hitchcock, Derek May, Lauren Moore, Victor Thompson, John Bennett and Britney Flannery. The remaining four of the twelve properties are owned by LLCs, so I will have to do some digging into those as well. I will have to follow up with Deputy May on these names and see if anything stands out to him.

Suddenly it hits me...Derek May? What is Deputy May's first name? I think back to when we first met and I don't think he ever gave it to me. Is it Derek? Why wouldn't he have told me that he lives so close to where Julia's necklace was found?

I decide to call Detective Ares and give him a heads up about the property owners in the area. I'm sure he has already done his digging in that aspect, but maybe he has a perspective on one of these names that I can look further into.

"Hey Morgen, how's everything going in the sticks?"

I can't help but roll my eyes and smirk. "Well, everything is just great...if you're into the whole Dateline special kind of thing."

Detective Ares laughs before responding, "I am a detective working many cases that deserve to be Dateline specials, so yeah, I guess I'm into that sort of thing."

"Fair enough. Speaking of, how is the Preston case going? I'm sure you are swamped since Meredith Stokes' body was found."

"Absolutely drowning in the swamp, Morgen. You know new cases don't wait to happen until you are done working the rest, which is why I am getting so much push back from my LT."

"Push back? How so?"

"They want me to redirect resources from the Preston case, Morgen. We just can't dedicate any more resources to the case with no new leads."

"What the fuck, are you serious? So, they would rather just wait to work her homicide then continuing to treat it as a possible rescue mission?"

"Did you already forget what this department is like? Lieutenant Samms' exact words were 'You'll be working the homicide eventually, you can dedicate resources then. For now, work the Stokes case and eventually the Preston girl's body will be found. Either by some hikers or some animal. The press is already forgetting the Preston girl, we need to get ahead on the Stokes case.' You know I don't agree, Morgen, but I can't go against his orders. All I can do is dedicate my personal time to the Preston case and hope we get a break soon."

The anger I feel bubbling inside me is threatening to spill over again. First it was Sheriff Marks. Now it's Lieutenant Samms. I am so sick of the toxic political bullshit getting in the way of helping people. Possibly saving someone's life. The never-ending flow of information we get now a days has made us all gluttons for the next thing. The next big story. The next big trend. We pretend to care until there is something else to care about. I can tell you who will never stop caring...the Preston family. The people whose lives now have a black hole that grows every day, sucking up everything in its path until there is no good, no joy, left to take. I can't just turn my back like everyone else. Someone has to keep pushing, to keep finding answers, even if the questions stop being asked.

"Ares, I'm not a cop anymore. I don't have to follow Lt. Samms or Minwall PD's bullshit orders anymore. I have been standing on the sidelines, hoping to assist you in finding Julia alive, but I will work this investigation like it's my own if you are now being told to stand down. I would never want to step on your toes, but I can't just give up on a victim. That's not why any of us got into this career."

"I was really hoping you would say that, Riley."

Chapter Thirty: Him

If I had it my way, my brother would be partnering with me in my business. Although I am clearly the better-looking brother, being twins means that he could find it equally simple to bait unsuspecting gazelles into his den. Our den. I've often imagined the amount of business we could pull working together. Unfortunately, he is perfectly fine working some bullshit job and taking care of our over the hill Pops, pretending to live a very fulfilling life. He is just as bad as the pathetic lives I extinguish.

At some point during our teenage years, he decided to discover mortality and shun anything he deemed unholy. Like he gets to decide what the fuck unholy is. I tried to appeal to the bond that exists solely because we are brothers, surprisingly he couldn't be swayed. It was the first time I actually saw him with a backbone. This was when I decided that I had to change. Not in the way that he wished, but instead by creating a mask that even he would never penetrate. I created a costume of normalcy, and discovered my true self in the unholiest of ways. At fifteen, I dressed in my costume and introduced my twin to the version of me that he wanted. All the while, my father nourished the version of me that my brother wanted to bury.

I learned many of the intricacies of this craft from my father. It's a shame that his body is becoming nothing more than a sack of potatoes in his old age because the man was brilliant. A brilliantly twisted sick fuck that I have looked up to since the first time I admitted to him the fantasies that filled my mind. My pathetic brother had told him everything. Every secret thought and fantasy that I assumed was safe when with my twin, my double. But it was unholy. Vile in the eyes of such a saint. Thankfully, my father is no saint. In fact, he was proud. I had never felt more seen or more celebrated by another human being than the day that my father discovered I was just like him.

I learned the beauty of my craft and the importance of my mask. Fast forward fifteen years later and I still practice my skills to perfection, and don my mask as if it is truly my own skin. My father taught me that my life could be everything I wanted it to be, and fuck anyone who stood in the way of that.

So once again my brother stands on his morality soap box, thinking he knows me so well. Once again, I will have to pacify him until everything blows over. And once again, it's me out here alone, having all the fun.

Chapter Thirty-One: Riley Morgen

I toss and turn in bed all night, going in and out of a fitful sleep, unable to stop thinking about Minwall Police Department quietly putting the Preston case on the backburner and a possible connection with Deputy May to this case. Why would he not mention that he lives near Binkin Trail? There has to be some innocent explanation for why he didn't think that information was important, right? If he were keeping it from me, why would he have given me a literal list of property owner names, knowing that he would be listed there? Maybe to appear more innocent, as if he just didn't think it was a big deal?

I decide to call Deputy May and ask him to meet me at The Conway for lunch. If I am going to start working this case like it is my own, I have to follow up on every name on my list... might as well start with the one I trust the most. I don't want to seem like I'm interviewing him...but I'm kind of interviewing him. Sure, I could ask all these questions over the phone, but it's important to see his face when he is answering the questions. There could be the smallest change in expression that would tell me so much more than his actual words ever could...and if it happens, I don't want to miss it.

I walk into The Conway ten minutes before noon and get a booth in the back of the main dining room. The building itself isn't large, but the dim lighting, high ceiling, massive wooden pillars and stone wall fireplace give the illusion of more room. The corner booth seems especially dimly lit, making me feel as if we'll have some actual privacy. At least, the illusion of privacy in a public restaurant. I slide into the booth and stare at the empty seat across from me. Almost a mental check that I can see well enough to catch any small changes in body language. I take a deep breath and steady myself, suddenly realizing that I am nervous. Why am I feeling nervous? This is Deputy May. The whole thing has to be a misunderstanding. In the short amount of time, I have known him, I trust him. He is a good cop, and a good man...there's no way he has anything to do with this...right? I am letting my imagination get the better of me, looking for answers everywhere and finding them nowhere. I have to stay focused. Once I talk to him, I can move past this suspicion and hopefully find some actual suspects in this list of property owners.

Deputy May arrives two minutes to noon and slides into the booth across from me, smiling warmly.

"Well, hello there, Miss Riley. Nice of you to invite me to lunch."

"Hello May. I have to admit there may be a bit of an ulterior motive to my invitation today."

"I wouldn't have expected anything less from you." He chuckles and begins scanning the menu in front of him casually. "Well, out with it. Might as well get business out of the way first."

"I just wanted to go over the names on the property list together. I figured you probably know everyone in this town and to me, it's just a list of strangers. Do you mind helping a newbie out?" I make sure to smile my 'please help me, I'm cute' smile, which earns me a laugh.

"Of course, Miss Riley, I had hoped you'd come to me if you needed any help."

From the dimly lit corner booth, I see a figure walking towards us, notepad in hand and silently praise the Lord for getting me one step closer to food in my stomach. As the server comes into the light hanging from the single lantern above our table, I realize the face is familiar.

"Hello Jack."

"Riley!", a set of gleaming teeth beam, nearly glowing white in this light, "It's been a while, how are you settling in?"

"Well Jack, thank you. I came in recently but you weren't working. Must have been your night off."

"Sorry I missed you." Jack begins, then glances towards Deputy May, as if suddenly noticing his presence. As he turns his face, I make mental note that the left side of his face is clean. No scar.

"Derek! Hey man, how you been?"

So, Deputy May is Derek May. Ok, one question confirmed without even having to ask. I didn't realize May and Jack were even friends, but I guess that's what you get in a small town. I should assume everyone knows everyone here...except for me.

"Doin' good, Jack. Doin' good. We'll have to catch up soon, but unfortunately, I'm working today. On my lunch break, so I'm just hopin' to grab a quick bite before I have to head back in."

"Of course, man, what can I get you both?"

Deputy May and I both order and Jack leaves us to it, with the promise of a quick return. I decide to take my opportunity to start getting a feel for Deputy May beyond just the brotherhood of the badge.

"I didn't realize I pulled you out here on your lunch break...sorry about that."

"Oh, don't you worry about that Miss Riley. I am on my lunch break, but there's no set time or rush. I was just sayin' that."

"Oh. Bad blood between you and Jack?"

"I wouldn't say all that. We've known each other since we were kids. Everyone that grew up here knows each other better than they even care to. There's just something off about both them boys."

"You mean Jack and Brady?"

"Yes ma'am. I've known 'em my whole life, but even as kids, we just kept our distance. Our dad didn't want us around the Bennett boys."

"I just met Brady recently at the hardware store. I thought Jack was playing a trick on me, it's weird he never mentioned he had a twin."

"Why is that weird? I have a twin too, Miss Riley."

Chapter Thirty-Two: Julia Preston

I can hear the calm, deep breaths of the other caged women. I am never sure what time it is anymore, but I know that I must be the first one awake today. Maybe it is early morning. I remember early mornings used to be so precious to me, the time where the whole world felt so calm and still. Like the earth itself wasn't quite awake yet, and I was given my own secret gift of extra time. Time to go for a run in the park, or make my favorite earl grey tea and sit on my balcony, watching the gentle morning light and breathing in the brand-new air. Each early morning I had was a blessing…something I will never be given again.

Every time I wake in this cage, I tell myself that I am blessed to still be breathing. Still be hunched on top of the dirt, instead of buried beneath it. I am blessed every time I leave this cage and go upstairs. I am blessed that the old man seems to want me alive…at least for now. I think about Elaine and how she can be okay after years of living like this. I dream of finding a way for us both to escape, to never be caged like animals again. Can I do this for years? Maybe all of this isn't so bad.

Suddenly I hear the familiar footsteps creaking down the steps. The breathing, slightly labored but almost soothing. The old man is coming. Is it my day today? Maybe I will be given something special today…enough food to stop the constant ache in my stomach. I hear the padding of his feet against dirt, walking towards the corner of this dirt prison. He must be getting the light. Is it my turn? I am almost giddy at the thought. The creak and squeal of the wheels as he rolls the light, it is heading in my direction. Oh, how I hope I can go upstairs today. I am so hungry.

I hear the familiar click of the light being turned on and involuntarily close my eyes, immediately blinded in my otherwise dark world. I can hear the rattle of the cage top, but it does not sound close enough. I don't feel the familiar shutter of the cage, the way the air suddenly changes, as if it too had been lying in wait for too long. I uncover my eyes, still pinched shut, and lower my face into the dirt. Nose touching the ground, I crack open one eye, staring down into the brown earth that I know as my personal penitentiary. I slowly turn my head, not daring to look too directly towards the light. I can see the old man's boots...near Elaine's cage. She is the only girl to my left; it must be her day. She is probably going to have another cheeseburger. Hell, maybe she'll have some fries and a milkshake too...might as well. I feel guilty at the immediate pang of jealousy in my gut. I shouldn't feel jealous of a woman who has been trapped here for years...so long she doesn't even remember. A woman who has no family to even notice she is missing, no family to look for her when she is gone.

I squeeze my eyes shut and force my nose back in the dirt between the bars of my cage floor. I hate myself for having even one bad thought about Elaine. She is everything to me here...well, her and the old man are all I have now. I have to rely on both of them now...just to stay alive.

Chapter Thirty-Three: Julia Preston

I have slept twice since I last spoke to Elaine. I'm starting to get very scared, since I have never seen a girl kept upstairs for even one night. Is Elaine dead? The thought brings tears to my eyes and nausea to my tiny hollow pit of a stomach. I can't lose her. I don't want to face this without her voice in the darkness, giving me comfort. I don't think I can do this without her. I can't stop the tears streaming down my cheeks, hot and steady, making mud of the ground beneath my face.

The sound of despair is not new to the walls of this makeshift prison. Somehow, I have become so immune to it, I find that the tears of the other girls soothe me to sleep most nights. Knowing that someone can still feel hope, even when turned into a caged animal, makes me believe we're all still human. I think I turned off the human side of me when I realized I was nothing more than an animal here, it was somehow just easier that way. Elaine understood that. Elaine kept me sane in a world where nothing is sane anymore. I will break without her...there will be no more pretending. Between a lack of food and the endless tears, I find myself suddenly very exhausted.

****

I wake to the sound of the door to the upstairs opening. The creak of the steps seems louder, heavier than usual. My senses

127

prick and burn with the creak, echoing in my ears and pounding in my head. Everything feels heavier without Elaine next to me...*Elaine.* Suddenly the empty cage beside me dawns on me all over again. Could the old man be bringing Elaine back down? Has Elaine finally come back to me?

All at once, I realize the sounds filling the dirt fortress are not those of Elaine or of the old man's steady breathing. It is the sound of dread, of doom, of the realization that your life is gone...it is the sound of a new girl...pleading. Her whimpering and begging for her life while the old man readies a new cage with nothing but the light of a headlamp.

A new girl.

No Elaine.

Elaine is gone.

She is dead.

Suddenly I want nothing more than to join her.

Chapter Thirty-Four: Riley Morgen

I spent the rest of lunch hearing Deputy May's opinions on each of the property owners on the list. He knew each of their lives in more detail than any neighbors in the city of Minwall ever would. I lived next to the same couple the entire eight years I lived in the city, and never once asked their names. I made sure to feign genuine surprise that I stumbled upon his name on the list...the last thing I want is to make him think I'm suspicious of him. Apparently, the house has been in his family for generations, each of the first-born men in his family named Derek May.

Based on Deputy May's neighborly knowledge, I have eliminated most of the people on the property owner list. Henry Michaels, Keegan Goode, Sean Hitchcock and Lauren Moore all grew up in this area and are well known by Deputy May. They went to school together, and most of their homes were passed down from deceased parents. Each of the four have families of their own...spouses and children that live in their homes with them. I really doubt Julia Preston is being hidden in a home with a spouse and children running around. I think it's safe to cross out those names.

Victor Thompson and Britney Flannery are both transplants to the area. Even though they didn't grow up here, they are both well known in the community. Victor is a firefighter who lives with his girlfriend, Kelly. Firefighters spend plenty of nights sleeping in the firehouse, so I would be surprised if Julia was hidden in Victor's house without

Kelly knowing. It is possible that Kelly could be in on the whole thing, but according to Deputy May, I'd be barking up the wrong tree with those two. They are his direct neighbors and he often watches the house for them when they go out of town, which is supposedly pretty often.

Britney Flannery is a second-grade teacher for Bearpoint Elementary who moved here from out of state a few years ago. She is a Sunday school teacher as well and spends her free time tutoring kids of all ages. There's no way she has children in and out of her house while holding a woman hostage.

The four properties owned by LLCs will still need researching. Deputy May brushed them off quickly, assuming that they are likely used as rental cabins for vacationing hikers. The explanation makes sense but I still need to confirm, hopefully with some simple online research.

The last two names are the ones that pique my interest the most. Derek May, who I will continue to keep an eye on. I want to trust him…I want to believe that I can still rely on my intuition when it comes to people. Law enforcement both hones that skill, and teaches you to never trust it completely. Never trust it so much that you become a fool.

The second name, John Bennett, is another that Deputy May knows well. John Bennett is the name of Jack and Brady's father…as well as the real name of Jack. It seems to be a thing in the country for the first-born sons to have a family name. Apparently, the Bennett family has lived in that home just as long as the May family has lived in theirs. There has been some unspoken rivalry between the two families since their grandfather's time. Deputy May did not go into detail about what the rivalry is all about, but he grew up knowing to not befriend the Bennett boys. A rivalry that deep deserves some looking into.

I sit at my kitchen table, updating my borderline suspects list.

Sheriff Marks – No new evidence on his prick ancestry; Did he leave the letter at my house?

Jack Bennett – Known to reside near the evidence discovery scene; Confirmed twin. Why does Deputy May not like him?

Brady Bennett – Known to reside near the evidence discovery scene; Confirmed twin. Why does Deputy May not like him?

Runner in the dark green joggers – Still need to identify. Possible cameras on any properties in the area?

Deputy May – Known to reside near evidence discovery scene; Same question as before: on my side or wants to be close to the investigation for information?

I feel restless reading the same names on my suspicious but not quite suspects list and decide that I can at least check for cameras on some of the properties near Binkin Trail.

I put on some running clothes, hoping to give myself a plausible excuse if I'm caught wandering around on someone's property, and head out for Binkin Trail.

Chapter Thirty-Five: Riley Morgen

I sprint with the most effort I can muster, hoping to get as drenched in sweat as possible, just in case I need to pretend I got lost while on a run. *Being new to the area, I had no idea this is private property*...as long as no one sees the property line map I now have folded up in my running fanny pack. I'm confident enough in my bullshitting skills to get away with some light trespassing.

When I see the spot where I discovered Julia's locket, I finally slow to a walk. I focus on catching my breath while I pull out the map from my running fanny pack. This exact spot is near the property line to homes owned by Keegan Goode and Sean Hitchcock. Each of the properties on this map seem to be very similar in shape and size. A long rectangle, somewhat narrow, each about sixteen acres or so in length. The homes tend to be located somewhere in the middle or front half of the property, with the large backyard areas backing up to Binkin Trail. I could imagine how easy it would be for someone to walk through numerous properties without ever being noticed...good for me today, bad for the suspect pool in this investigation.

I glance around as casually as I can, then leave the dirt path, walking toward the first property that lines this site...Keegan Goode. I am not so naïve that I assume I'm going to stumble upon some other piece of evidence laying on the ground. No, this mission is specifically for cameras. The most likely scenario in this area would be trail cams. I plan to walk the backs of these properties as far as I can, just doing some scouting for trail cams. I'm interested to see if I am the only person using the dense woods of these private properties to get around instead of an actual road.

As much as I would like to cover the area quickly, I instead choose to go slow and steady, visually checking every tree trunk, every ruffled area of leaves. Although I don't expect to find anything, but hopefully a trail cam, I want to use this time to get as much area covered as possible. The more thoroughly I check the area, the less likely I will have any questions that cause me to have to check it again. The second, less likely reason I also want to take it slow, is the possibility that someone else is out here right now. The woods tend to have a certain peaceful quiet, even with all the little creatures going about their days. I want to add as little noise as possible to this peace, just in case I need to hear the crunching of footsteps on leaves that do not belong to me.

After what feels like hours, I have cleared Keegan Goode's property and am well into Sean Hitchcock's. With no luck yet, I stop and check the property map, curious where I will be trespassing next. The next will be Britney Flannery, the school teacher. After that, a property owned by Deer Keep LLC. That sounds like a hunter, which hopefully means a trail cam. I quickly zip up my map into my fanny pack and begin the slow trek again, eager to get as much area searched as possible before nightfall.

About forty minutes later, I am near the end of Sean Hitchcock's invisible property line when I glance ahead of me, mentally preparing for the next property. I stop hard in my tracks. A short distance from me, off to my left, I see a box on the trunk of a tree. My heart beat immediately quickens as I

133

rush over to verify my findings. This is the rush I miss when finding evidence on a crime scene…there is nothing more satisfying than finding each of the puzzle pieces, fitting them together perfectly to see the whole picture. Softly dropping to my knees, I grab the trail cam and open the box. I can't believe my luck. This model has a playback screen, meaning I won't have to steal an SD card, or awkwardly approach the property owner requesting access to that game cam I saw while trespassing on their property.

First things first…I delete the images of me approaching the camera just moments ago. Definitely don't need any evidence that Sheriff Marks could end up using against me. It may just be a little light trespassing, but that prick would jump at the chance to charge me with anything right now. When I left the Sheriff's Office, he probably looked up every state code, completely shocked that a woman talking back to a man isn't an arrestable offense. Or maybe I'm giving him too much credit that he would care to actually look into state codes. He probably went straight to a magistrate and tried to get a warrant on me…felony woman not knowing her place charge. I roll my eyes and focus on the trail cam…the quicker I get this done, the better.

I begin clicking through the available photos, seeing as many deer as I would have expected in this area. I click fast, not wanting to be caught in the middle of something I can't lie my way out of, all my focus on the screen, not wanting to miss anything of importance. All I hear is my own breathing, heavy with anticipation, and the soft *click click click* of the trail cam's next button. Suddenly, like a bomb going off next to me, the snap of a twig reverberates across the woods. I hold my breath, careful not to make a sound, as I look around for the source of the noise. The forest is dense, my view limited to the area directly around me. I wait, exercising as much patience as I can muster, slowly scanning the area and coming up with no source to blame the sound on. The sudden stillness of the forest surrounding me makes the hair on the back of my neck rise. I am not alone. This I know, but my eyes aren't bringing me any evidence of this fact.

I hurriedly continue clicking through the photos, suddenly wanting nothing more than to finish this task and get back to Binkin Trail. How many freaking deer has this thing seen? Has every deer in the state of Virginia done a parade through Sean Hitchcock's property? I glance around continuously, convinced that I am being watched and refusing to be snuck up on. My fingers suddenly stop, as if having a mind of their own. I see two figures on the small playback screen. I quickly take out my phone and snap a picture of the screen. I click the back button, then click my phone's photo button. Again, again, again. Back to the deer parade. I have seen enough, I can't stay knelt here like prey, and I can't leave possible evidence to be destroyed. I power down the trail cam and pop the SD card out, quickly putting it in my runner's fanny pack. The last thing I wanted to do was commit a petite larceny, but I can't chance leaving this here. The hair on the back of my neck is standing stick straight...*I know I am being watched.* I close the trail cam and stand up, walking towards Britney Flannery's property as casually as if I belong.

I am barely breathing as I will every sense to stay on edge. I hear another twig snap, sounding closer than I expected. Instead of giving anyone the upper hand, letting them know I was aware of their presence, or chancing turning around to see them...I break into a full sprint. I know I am fast, and the terrain gives me the upper hand of being able to weave between trees, much harder to grab given the chance that my stalker is also fast. Suddenly, the dense trees begin to thin out and I see what must be the invisible line drawn between Britney Flannery's property and part of Binkin Trail. I leap over that invisible line and am suddenly in the open, feeling both relieved and very exposed. I spin around and look to the wood line, seeing and hearing nothing. I clutch my fanny pack instinctively, knowing the SD card is safe.

I start to walk Binkin Trail, heading toward my house, catching my breath and trying my best to look like I'm any other runner...not nearly someone's prey in the woods.... or someone who just trespassed and stole possible evidence in the case of a missing woman. Up ahead I see a figure near the wood line, starting to walk up the trail. Did he just come out of the woods? I didn't actually see him leave the woods but why else would you be off the trail, right near the wood line? He's walking towards me now, still too far off to see any features. I work hard at calming my breath...is this who was watching me on Sean Hitchcock's property?

As the man gets closer, I recognize the face, but don't immediately know the name. The attractive face smiles in recognition of me, then slightly turns, checking the wood line. As he turns, I see the unmistakable scar above the chiseled jaw line.

"Hello Riley."

"Hello Brady, surprised to see you out here."

"Are you?" He smiles, but this time I feel a chill down my sweat lined back. "I'm an avid runner, I'm out here quite often, actually. Binkin Trail is so peaceful." He then looks me up and down, which does nothing to calm the way my skin is prickling. "It seems you agree with me. I didn't know you were a runner."

"I am, I'm quite fast actually."

"Hmm, maybe we will have to race sometime. I've been told I'm pretty fast myself."

He's playing with me now…we both know that we were not out here for a good work out. We both know that we were in those woods. What does Brady have to do with this? Why would he care what I have to do with this? Why do I feel a prickling sensation on every part of my skin when he speaks? When he looks at me? Our eyes are locked, both testing each other to break from this little game.

"Maybe we will, Brady."

"I look forward to it, Riley Morgen." With this, he smiles that same smile that started my skin prickling. How can someone so good looking come off so incredibly creepy? He begins to walk away, humming to himself like we just had an immensely pleasant conversation.

I wait until he is no longer in sight, then I sprint the entire way home. Even after locking the door behind me, I can't shake the sickening feeling Brady Bennett gives me.

Chapter Thirty-Six: Julia Preston

The new girl has been here for days...maybe a week now, I don't know. I have not spoken to her, just listened to her whimpering, her sobbing in the refusal to accept her new reality. She is not *breaking*; she is going to die soon.

I have not spoken since Elaine left. What is the point in connecting with these girls in this cell? In this prison, no one leaves alive. I cannot love these girls and let my soul die piece by piece every time one of them never returns. When I first got here, all I wanted was to live...what a cruel joke it is to call this a life.

Many hours after waking, the old man descends the stairs. A flash of thought in my mind has me thinking it may be the new girl's time to never return. At least the whimpering will stop soon. Even in my sorrow, I feel a deep pang of guilt at my callous thoughts. None of these girls deserve this...but hope is not my friend anymore. It is a stranger that insists we have a past...a past that I no longer remember.

The spotlight is on me today; I should be excited to go upstairs. Upstairs is the only place that feels somewhat human anymore. I will be given food, even a handful of candy is everything here...it is life. I don't even know that I want life anymore...not this...this is not life. Wrists, legs and waist chained, I am led upstairs and locked in the kitchen chair. The old man walks to the kitchen, making his tray as usual. I don't even bother watching, fear of the unknown is nonexistent when I have already accepted death as a welcome friend.

He sits in front of me, staring into my eyes, looking almost human. If I didn't know who this man was, I would never believe he is capable of this. I want to cry and scream, begging for Elaine and for our lives, but I instead remind myself to not be fooled. This man is not human...no matter how deep his eyes look, how soft his features sit, filled with concern.

"My Julia..." He strokes my cheek and lightly caresses my hair before continuing, "You seem so sad. I hate to see you like this; this is not you. Where is my sweet sunshine?"

"Why did you take Elaine from me?"

My brashness seems to surprise him, I have never shown this side of myself, never questioned his actions directly. I expect to be struck, punished for questioning the man who is now in control of me, my life in his hands. I expect to be thrown back into my cage, hungry and battered to rot for another week. I expect to never see my cage again, a new girl replacing me, my memory forever tainted by this cabin in the woods.

Instead, the corners of his lips turn upwards, a smile emerging. I am thankful he keeps his mouth closed, his smile appearing almost appealing, trustworthy, without his rotten teeth being presented.

"I'm so sorry if I have worried you, Julia. Elaine is here. She is fine."

The shock must register on my face because the old man chuckles. I don't know if I can believe him, if this is some trick, or some fucked up way of saying her spirit will always be with us. I wait for him to continue, unable to speak for fear of giving in to hope's wicked game.

"You know what, Julia...Elaine said I can trust you...and I think she's right. I think it's time we test that."

The old man lifts the tray from the table, about ten crackers and a few candies on a paper plate, disappearing back into the kitchen. I hear the opening of a refrigerator then the buzz of a microwave. Instantly, a burst of smell fills the living room. My mouth immediately watering, drool nearly falling from my lips, I recognize the smell of grilled meat and cheese. It is so overwhelming, I feel tears pooling in my eyes. My body silently begs for the nourishment I have lacked for weeks, months, years…I don't even know how long I have wasted away.

The old man returns with his tray, this time gleaming with a cheeseburger and fries. He sits in front of me, again showing a closed mouth smile while stroking my arm, and begins to speak.

"You have not eaten properly in months. That can change now, Julia. It is up to you. I am extending my trust to you. I will provide for you…everything you need to live a good life. I will allow you to stay upstairs, to not return to the basement. I will allow you to stay with Elaine. These privileges are not without your cooperation. There will be a lot expected of you, but for now, baby steps. Today, I want to feed you properly. I want you to remain upstairs, in one of the bedrooms, with Elaine. I want to give you the world Julia, because I love you. Elaine loves you. We are a family now, correct?"

"Yes, we are family. I love you and I love Elaine, too." The words escape my mouth without any thought. They sound so foreign in my own ears, but I do not stop them. I am not even sure if I meant them or am in a trance induced by the smell of real food. *It somehow felt so right letting those words leave my mouth.* I swallow hard and keep my focus on the old man.

140

The mouth full of rot makes an appearance. He looks so genuinely happy, I think I might be smiling too. "I'm so happy for all of us, my sweet sunshine. Let's share this burger, then I'll take you to Elaine. She has missed you too."

As he feeds me my half of cheeseburger, hot rolling tears stream down my cheeks. I have no idea if they are from the shock of real food, knowing Elaine is alive, or the idea of a new family.

Chapter Thirty-Seven: Him

I'm starting to question if my meddling brother is right in worrying about that cop, Riley Morgen. It seems that she is having a hard time keeping her nose out of the old man's business. I am not concerned about my business being exposed, that will never happen. But if the old man goes down, people in Bearpoint and Minwall suddenly become more aware...and that is simply not good for business.

Don't get me wrong, I don't plan on helping the bastard. He's got enough experience with this shit; it's up to him to cover his own tracks. He must know it's time to lay low since I haven't heard any new orders from him in months. It's not typical of the bastard.

I, on the other hand, am not worried about laying low at the moment. In fact, I'm already starting to think about the next experiment I want to perform. I'm not quite itching for the next test subject yet, but I know it will come soon enough. It always does. I might as well enjoy the buildup of the fantasy while I wait. In the meantime, life goes on as usual. Which means three things occupying much of my time...my real business, the job that allows me to blend in with society, and my dad.

I have convinced my brother that my job takes up enough of my time that he covers the majority of my dad's care. It's pretty fucked up when you think about it...even as my brother handles most of Dad's needs, I'm still the favorite. I am still the one that Dad wants to spend his time with, have conversations with. I know that must eat at my brother. Good. Serves him right for thinking he has some moral high ground on me. Pretty funny that the thing my brother wants to kill in me, is the thing that Dad loves the most.

I am proud that I got to see my dad in his truest form growing up. I got to see him work, and I got to learn from the best. He was truly someone to fear before old age started ravaging his body. Luckily, his mind is still the same. Still that same sick fuck who salivates at my stories of bloodshed and final moments filled with sheer terror. No matter the story, he always ends the conversation the same way. "That's my boy." I have been his boy since he found out that I am just like him. See, that's the piece my brother is missing. That single piece that just never locked into place for him. Sad, really.

Today is an unusual day off for me, from both my bullshit job and my real business. I am spending the day with Dad while my brother works the bullshit job that he pretends gives him purpose.

After lunch, I tell Dad every detail of my little whore skinning experiment and he is thrilled.

"I can't believe you didn't invite your old man. I know I'm more of a liability than an asset with the wild ones but I would have loved to watch. You could at least give me that."

I laugh. Even in his aging body, my dad still has such a love for our craft. I hope to be just like him one day...but if I am lucky, my body will fare well enough to keep perfecting the art well into my sixties.

"You know I would Dad...if watching eyes wouldn't be questioning where you were."

"I know, I know...the mistake."

"I don't know that he could be called a mistake when we are twins, Dad. Without him, there could have been no me."

"We should have just had one. You."

"No use crying over a split egg, Dad."

I don't blame my dad for his feelings, or lack of, for my twin. I too, share a lack of feelings when it comes to that sheep. But I at least have the decency to not be quite so open and honest about it. I have always believed that one day, he will prove his worth. I have been waiting a long time with no luck so far, but one day, maybe he will finally get his chance.

Chapter Thirty-Eight: Riley Morgen

My closet door is open and boxes scattered across the bedroom; I sit on the floor searching in yet another stuffed moving box. Yes, I am ashamed to admit that I still have a number of moving boxes hiding away in my closet. I would complain about the number of belongings I have, but I will be incredibly thankful for my pack rat tendencies when I find the SD card reader, I know I have somewhere in here. It was just another random tool I acquired while working patrol, needing to download photos from a GoPro attached to a helmet after a bicyclist was injured in a hit and run. In this case, it could help me identify the people in the trail cam photos, and possibly even get me one step closer to finding Julia Preston.

Ah, ha!

I pull the SD card reader from the bottom of one of several boxes filled with things I acquired during policing. I jump up and scurry into the kitchen, plopping down in front of my laptop at the kitchen table. Once everything is setup and I am opening the folder, seconds from seeing the trail cam photos, I feel a rush of excitement. I could be one step closer to getting some real answers about Julia Preston. Why was her locket found here in Bearpoint? Is she being held here? Is she still alive? Is it her in these trail cam photographs?

It takes a few minutes of scrolling through the pictures of deer to find the few that actually have people in them. Now that the image is on a computer screen, I am able to see it much more clearly, especially in full screen mode. Most of these pictures do not show any faces, either faces pointing towards the ground as they walk, or heads turned behind them...almost like they are worried about being followed. One photo shows the two figures, one clad in a black sweatshirt and jeans, hood pulled up over the head; the other wearing a short skirt and a tank top, high heels on her feet. The date on the photo, assuming the camera clock is programmed correctly, shows four days ago at 4:16am. Suddenly I realize that both of these figures are women. Although it's hard to tell with the one clad in a big sweatshirt, the height is similar, or likely smaller than, to the skirt clad woman next to her, which does not seem tall in relation to where the trail cam sat on the tree. The sweatshirt wearing figure also has skinny legs, but more of a womanly figure in the hips.

The two women seem to be dressed as polar opposites. Not that it is impossible for friends to have different styles, but the woman in a skirt is dressed as if she would be going out to a club...not for a walk in the woods. I am able to see her face, but she does not seem familiar. At the very least, it isn't Julia Preston. Is the woman in the hoodie Julia? Is it possible that Julia isn't a victim at all, just running from her old life?

I continue scrolling through pictures and realize there are more with the hooded woman. The time stamp is showing the same date, with a time of 1:40am. This time, hoodie is alone. She is walking the opposite direction, away from the trail cam. Okay, so whoever this is...she was going to pick up the other woman at nearly two in the morning, walking through the woods? That seems really unusual. I continue scrolling through the multiple still shots of this woman's back as she was walking through Sean Hitchcock's property, toward

146

Binkin Trail. The final photo before she is nearly out of view, she is glancing behind her, right cheek over her shoulder, showing a decent profile of the side of her face. I zoom in as much as I can, but the detail is not great. Still, she seems familiar. There is no hair showing, just a grainy view of half of her face. Even with nothing more than that, I can say two things for certain.

The hoodie wearing wanderer is a woman...and something is telling me I know her.

Chapter Thirty-Nine: Julia Preston

When I had finished eating, the old man took me to a room in the back of the cabin. The room was windowless and dark, two small beds on opposite walls, the way two children's shared bedroom would be arranged. It had a small bathroom attached, with a real toilet and a bath tub. There were no decorations on the walls, no soft rugs or carpeting on the hard floor, and no lamps to provide guidance in the dark. Each bed had a single pillow and a single blanket. It was a very basic room, fulfilling the very basic needs of a human being.

It was the most beautiful thing I had ever laid eyes on.

It was clear Elaine had missed me too. We lay together, in a single tiny bed, huddled under one blanket, clutching to each other like young sisters terrified of a booming thunderstorm looming outside our nonexistent window. Her breath in my ear so familiar and comforting, I felt like I was home. We didn't speak a word the first night we were reunited.

The first few days in this room felt like a dream. I sometimes wasn't sure if I would wake up in my cage, only to find Elaine still had not returned. Maybe it was all some starvation induced hallucination. Waking up today, I again will myself to believe that this is real. I sit up in my bed, rubbing at my wrists, flinching as I touch the raw, warped skin. It still feels strange to not be handcuffed or chained. My wrists and ankles never became used to the constant friction of metal, the flesh in red rings of open sores and hard patches of skin. I look over to see Elaine still sleeping peacefully, her gray fleece blanket draped around her.

While this room is windowless, I am able to tell the difference between day and night in here. Sometimes it is almost overwhelming, the difference a small amount of light makes when you have become so used to the blackest dark. In the cage, I felt like I knew Elaine so well…I felt as though she was my sister. I wanted to die without her, but I had never even seen her. I knew her voice as if I had been hearing it all my life, but I could not tell you what color hair she had, or eyes…or if she was tall or short. None of those things mattered, I loved her all the same.

This room allowed me to finally see Elaine. She is exactly who I expected…but with the benefit of knowing her heart first. Elaine is a small woman, just under average height, but very thin. I blame the conditions of living here, but who knows if she took any care of herself before being here either. Based on the width of my wrists as I gently rub them, I know I must be a sickly thin version of myself right now too. Elaine's hair is deep brown, near black, and she keeps it in a thick braid all the time. Her eyes are a beautiful amber colored brown that reminds me of a rich, sticky honey that my mom used to buy at the farmers market when I was growing up. It is clear in her face that she has lived a rougher life than I have ever known. Elaine bears scars both physically and unseen. Though her features are conventionally beautiful, a life of suffering and drug use has stolen the beauty that likely once shone through. I can still see it. Maybe that was the benefit of knowing her heart before ever seeing her face.

149

I rise from my bed quietly, feet softly padding on the hard floor, and close the door to the bathroom. It is a luxury that still feels unreal…using the bathroom like a normal person. I take a bath everyday now. There is no soap or shampoo, no conditioner or bubble bath. There is hot water…and that is more than enough. Before coming to this room, I had not bathed since coming to the old man. I spent the entire first bath crying from the overwhelming relief the hot water gave me while Elaine gently rubbed my skin with a washcloth. The water looked like mud when she was finished.

It is strange that I am happy again. I am happy here. I am clean and I eat. I have Elaine and the old man is good to us. This is starting to feel like my home and my family. I still miss my real family, especially my mom…but somehow it feels like this is okay. Everything will be okay.

Sometimes I wonder if I have truly broken…not just pretend anymore.

Then the little voice in my head reminds me… we are no longer caged, no longer chained, but we are still prisoners.

I try not to let myself forget that.

Chapter Forty: Riley Morgen

I email the best picture of the hooded woman to Detective Ares, asking if she seems familiar to him in any way. If I can at least determine why this girl seems so familiar to me, maybe I can determine if the late-night walk in the woods is suspicious or completely unrelated. I should bring it to Deputy May too, but I worry about showing him for two reasons. One, I should not have been snooping around on Sean Hitchcock's property without his permission, and I damn sure should not have taken his trail cam's SD card. I really don't want to have to answer any questions about where these photos came from.

Two...I still don't know if I can trust Deputy May. My paranoia is probably completely unwarranted but I don't know who I can trust in Bearpoint yet. Deputy May lives so close to where the locket was found, and I'm convinced the key to all of this is the location of that locket. Why would the locket be on Binkin Trail, over 40 miles from where Julia Preston's last known location is? If Deputy May were involved in it, why would he have provided me the list of property owners surrounding Binkin Trail? I could have gotten the information myself, so it could have just been a ploy to seem helpful...keep him under the radar. Or maybe I am overthinking all of this, and Deputy May could be the only one I actually can trust in Bearpoint.

After allowing the joys of overthinking to overtake me for long enough, I decide I don't have any options but to keep

Deputy May on my side for now. If he really is involved in all of this, it will become clear to me eventually. But for now, I am better off with an ally in Bearpoint. Which means, I need to show him the picture.

****

A few hours later Deputy May and I sit at my kitchen table, laptop open and papers scattered around us.

"Let me show you something." I pull the laptop closer to me and open the picture of the hooded woman on Sean Hitchcock's property. Flipping the laptop toward Deputy May, I speak again, "Do you recognize this woman?"

Deputy May takes a hard look, squinting at the screen, before he speaks. "I don't recognize her, Miss Riley. I don't think she lives in Bearpoint, I would have seen her at some point if she did."

Spinning the laptop toward myself again, I open the other photos and find the best view of the woman in the skirt's face. "What about this woman?"

Deputy May again thoughtfully studies the photo; eyes squinted and face scrunched. "I've never seen her before. She certainly doesn't look dressed to be in the woods though."

"I thought the same thing. They both seem entirely out of place."

"Where was this photo taken?"

"Near Binkin Trail." I respond quickly, pretending to study the papers in front of me. I'm hoping Deputy May will drop it without any more questions. I would rather not lie to him if possible.

"There are no cameras on the trail. Did you get this from someone's property?"

Ugh. I did not expect such a direct question, a lie unavoidable. I guess I should have given May more credit...he is a cop. "It did come from someone's property."

"Miss Riley, please don't tell me you took this from someone's trail cam?"

I stare at Deputy May, the silence between us growing.

I have lied plenty of times in my life. Most of these with a good-natured purpose behind it. I have lied to suspects during interrogations...made them believe I was on their side, or pretended I believed them over the victim. Those types of lies built rapport. Those types of lies are sometimes necessary if you want someone to eventually tell the truth about the crimes they have committed. I have lied to my mother when I tell her that I am fine. A lie that comes from a good place, not wanting my mom to worry unnecessarily.

This lie just feels like I'm lying to a friend for no good reason. A friend that I partially think could be a suspect, but still. This lie feels dirty.

"May, I am keeping you out of the details that you don't need to know. Not because I don't trust you but because I want to protect you...and your job. I hope you understand that."

Deputy May's eyes widen and he lowers his voice, as if we have to worry about eavesdroppers in the privacy of my kitchen. I'm sure the deer are looking in the windows right now, making notes to take right to the sheriff.

"Don't be getting yourself in trouble, Miss Riley. The sheriff is looking for a reason to make things hard on you right now...don't make it easy for him."

"I promise to make that bastard work for it."

At least that earned me a smile.

As the night went on, the piles of papers became messier, but I was no closer to finding any answers. I start to think sleep would do me better than the endless what if theories May and I went back and forth about for the last couple of hours. As I rise from the table, about to let May know I am ready to get to bed, his whole-body stills, eyes glued to a notebook in his hands.

"What is this?"

A nauseating wave of realization nearly makes my knees buckle. It is my private notebook, where my list of potential suspects is. What is it doing in the piles on the kitchen table? I swear I put it in my nightstand drawer, where I always keep it. I'm stalling, trying to think on my feet of how I can answer to his name being on that list, someone that calls me a friend.

"It's just notes from when I first started looking into Julia's disappearance. I haven't even looked at it in a month or more." I try to grab the notebook, but Deputy May stands too, moving his hand so that the notebook is no longer in my reach.

"I'm a suspect? You really think I could have abducted a woman?"

Caught.

Crap.

Like a deer in headlights. The car barreling toward me and I am too shocked to move.

"No, May. I just had to list everyone that could have been related to this in any way. I don't actually think you are involved in this."

I'm sure he can see my brain is scrambling now. I never wanted him to see that list. Why is my paranoid brain like this? Why must I be unable to see genuine good in someone?

He lifts the notebook to his face and reads my own words, using them against me like weapons, guns in a fist fight. "On my side or wants to be close to the investigation for information?"

He looks me in the eyes, slowly lowering his hand. For a minute, I don't breathe. He's a cop...he will understand, right? He knows every possible suspect has to be eliminated during an investigation. It is nothing personal. He gets that, right?

"Are you really that damaged by this career that you can't see when someone is on your side? You can't see when someone actually cares about you? I am risking my career by helping you, Riley. I thought we were friends, but a friend would know that I wouldn't ever hurt someone else. Especially a woman. I can't believe you would think otherwise."

Okay, maybe he doesn't get the whole it's not personal thing. "May, I'm sorry. I swear it wasn't like that; it was-"

Deputy May cuts me off, "You've already insulted me once. Don't do it again with lies and excuses." He throws the notebook onto the table and heads for the front door.

I'm scrambling to think of what to say. I have nothing. I can't excuse this. It was a shitty thing to do to someone who never gave me a reason to mistrust him. I'm following behind him like a child, telepathically begging him to hear me out...not to leave. Finally, I find my voice, "Derek, please. Let me explain."

155

"I think it's best that you don't, Riley. Why don't you take some time to figure this investigation out on your own? Don't let me muddy it up."

He opens the door and steps outside, glancing back before leaving me with his final words, "Until I'm officially off that list…don't bother calling me."

I stand on the porch watching him leave, feeling like the smallest person on this planet. Did I totally just fuck that up? I think I might be watching the one friend I had walk out of my life for good. Maybe I am that damaged. Maybe he is right.

As I turn to walk back inside, I catch something white in my peripheral vision. I think I feel my neck crack at the speed which my head whips around. For a moment, I think my heart beat has paused as I stare at the envelope laying near the steps of my front porch. Feeling suddenly very alone, I grab the envelope and casually walk inside. I refuse to give into the anxiety prickling at my neck, screaming at me to run inside and lock the doors.

Once I am safely back in my house, envelope in hand, I lock the doors and make sure all the window shades are closed. I sit at the kitchen table, pushing the mountain of useless papers away with such force, half of them go floating across the room. I rip open the envelope, not giving a fuck about gloves or possible evidence. Who would send it to a lab for me anyway? Deputy May sure isn't interested in being involved in anything Riley related right now. Not that I blame him. As I unfold the white, unlined paper, I again see one typed line in the middle of the page.

"You are going to need more than one deputy on your side, Riley Morgen. I am getting tired of warnings."

156

I am so angry at myself. I am so angry at this career for taking away my trust. I am so angry at myself for letting my hurt, hurt someone else. And as much as I feel for everything that just happened between me and Deputy May...I am even more angry that someone thinks they can come on my property to threaten me.

I am not a cop anymore...and I am sick of following the rules and policies that governed me for years.

Fuck it. I'm going rouge.

Chapter Forty-One: Julia Preston

I sit on my bed, gray flannel blanket wrapped around my shoulders, letting myself start to drift into the tiredness that usually comes around this time of night. The click of the bathroom door opening brings me back to consciousness, expecting to see Elaine crawling into her bed. Instead, I see that she is dressed in clothes I have never seen before.

"What are you doing? Where did you get those clothes?"

"The old man gave 'em to me. I have to do some work for him tonight."

"Work? Elaine…what are you talking about?"

Elaine looks exhausted. She sits on her bed, sighing heavily, never breaking eye contact.

"Julia, we aren't living in the upstairs because he likes us. No matter who says they love you…love always has a price."

"What is the price, Elaine?"

"He says you aren't ready for the next stage yet…and you should be happy about that. I won't be able to shield you forever…please just let me do it for a little while longer."

I don't know what to say to that. I feel sick to my stomach with worry…but not for myself, for Elaine. Is he hurting her? Is he raping her? How could she take all of this burden on her shoulders and never even tell me? I feel terrible…she is the big sister I have never had in so many ways.

"Fix your face, Julia. Don't ever waste time worrying about me. I am a big girl, and nothing that happens to me here is any worse than what used to happen to me when I was living

158

on the streets of Minwall. The big difference here is that I have you. Someone I actually give a fuck about. I don't think I ever had that before."

My heart aches. I desperately want to trade places with Elaine, and I don't even know what I would be volunteering for. Before I can speak, Elaine stands and starts a determined stride to the door. She raises her hand in a fist in front of the door then turns toward me, her amber eyes locking with mine.

"Seriously, don't worry Jules. I will be back by the time you wake up."

Elaine turns to face the door again and knocks loudly. A few minutes later I hear the locks turning, loudly reminding me of its presence, the simple device that keeps us labeled under the name of prisoner. I want to say something. I want to scream and beg Elaine to stay. I want to beg the old man to hurt me instead; to give Elaine the rest she has never had in her life. Before I can do any of these things, the door opens and Elaine leaves the room, not looking back at my tear-filled eyes.

The door clicks shut, locks loudly clicking in place one by one.

I am a coward.

Hot tears stream down my face. I feel alone and so angry with myself. How can I let this happen to someone I love while I lay here in a bed sleeping? What about all the girls still in those cages, downstairs? I can't let myself forget what is happening here. I have been so thankful to feel okay in the last few days, to eat and bathe, to sleep in a bed and have Elaine to talk to. I almost let myself forget that we are not the only prisoners here.

I have to hold on to myself...sometimes I think there is so little left.

Chapter Forty-Two: Riley Morgen

I open my eyes to see my handgun laying on the bed in front of me, my fingers still wrapped around the grip, fingertip pads pressing tightly into the front strap. Surprisingly, the nightmares didn't haunt me last night, but it's likely because I was in and out of sleep all night. Every branch creaking outside sent chills down my spine, convincing myself that a new letter would be waiting for me on my porch. Each time I closed my eyes; I saw the look of hurt on Deputy May's face. I guess it haunted my sleep enough that my brain decided I didn't need the nightmares for one night.

Lifting myself slowly out of bed, I realize how stiff and sweaty I feel. I need a hot shower and a good plan. Sitting at home stewing inside my head is not an option today. This is deeper than some exercise therapy will soothe. I feel terrible about hurting Deputy May. He's the one friend I have in Bearpoint and I am suddenly feeling very alone. I thought I preferred a solitary life, but this is a loneliness that makes me question ever leaving the city. Would I feel this way if our friendship wasn't real? I doubt it. Could our friendship be real and he still be responsible for Julia Preston's disappearance? Is the whole friendship just his way of staying off the radar? I hate that I can feel like such a jerk for writing that damn list and still feel like I can't be sure that Deputy May shouldn't be on that list.

161

After showering and getting dressed, I lace up my sneakers with plans to go into town and get something to eat. If I fuel up at The Conway, hopefully I will see Jack and be able to dig a little deeper into the relationship between the Bennett boys and Derek May. Considering Jack is on my suspect list; it doesn't hurt to get to know him better too.

The drive into town is always a reminder of why I chose to live in Bearpoint. The pine lined road seems to hide me from the rest of the world and brings a sense of peace that I am in desperate need of right now. The fifteen minutes of peace is more than I have felt all night. It is just enough to clear out my head and prepare me for another round of secret interviewing.

Absentmindedly, I park in front of the hardware store and gather my things from the passenger seat. As I lift my gaze, I stop suddenly as my eyes lock with Brady Bennett's. He is standing in the hardware store window, wearing a tan carpenter apron, staring at me with no expression on his face. I feel the hair on the back of my neck lifting. Even as it is clear that I see him watching me, he does not move. He wants me to know he is watching. I feel suddenly very exposed. I want out of this exchange, this feeling, and my body is telling me to get away.

As I walk towards The Conway, I glance again towards the hardware store and see that Brady has now turned his body toward me, eyes still locked and following, no expression crossing his perfectly chiseled face. I fight the shiver that tries to take over my body and refuse to look away from his gaze until he is out of view. There is something off about that man, but I refuse to let him see how much he creeps me out.

I pull open the heavy wooden door to The Conway and stride straight for the bar. I forget all about the creepy twin experience as I see Jack wiping down the bottles of liquor that line the back wall. How can two people from the same egg be so different personality wise? They are mirror images of each other, minus Brady's scar, but the feeling I get from the two of them is worlds apart.

Jack turns, noticing me sitting at the bar, and smiles broadly.

"Hey Riley, how's it going?"

I return the warm smile. I am going to need to loosen him up a bit, and hopefully get something useful to this investigation.

"Hey Jack! Everything is going well, just finally settling into the new place and soaking up all the nature possible. How have you been?"

"Same ole, same ole. Just been working. Speaking of…what can I get you today?"

After I place my order, Jack continues cleaning his area and making small talk with me. I can feel that he has started to relax into our conversation, though he seems a bit distracted. I am not sure if he has something on his mind, or is just focusing on the things he needs to get done behind the bar. The restaurant is nearly empty, as I had hoped it would be, coming in before the lunch rush. Jack tends to one table in the corner then returns to the bar. I decide to jump into some deeper conversation, hoping to seem as casual as possible.

"I met your brother recently. I had no idea you had a twin."

"Oh, Brady? Yeah, twins in looks alone." Jack laughed before continuing, "We are such different people, but I love the weirdo."

163

"Yes, I did notice that you seem very different. I thought you were playing a trick on me at first, then realized that no one is that good of an actor."

Jack chuckles again, seeming very amused at my initial confusion. "He's a good man; he's just a bit unusual."

"No kidding." I regret it as soon as I let it slip. I glance up and see that Jack is still smiling, seemingly not offended that I basically just called his brother a freak.

I decide to change the subject quickly, and hope that I haven't made Jack question this budding friendship in any way.

"Deputy May told me that he grew up with you and Brady."

The smile vanishes from Jack's face. I am taken back by the sudden harshness of his handsome features. This is a side of Jack's emotions I have not yet seen. I think I hit a nerve.

"Yeah, Derek and his brother Jordan grew up down the street from us. I wouldn't say we were close though. Our families have some history so our dad always told us to stay away from the May boys."

Interesting. So, both sets of twins grew up being told to avoid the other. That's a family feud that must run deep...I'm sure there's a story there. Not that I'm going to prod into that right now...I don't want to make Jack close himself off completely.

"Oh. Does Jordan still live around here too?"

"Oh yeah. They both still live in the house they grew up in... I think their dad still lives there too."

Chapter Forty-Three: Riley Morgen

I return home to hear the ping of a new email spring from my cell phone. I see Detective Ares' name and click excitedly, hoping for some answers about the woman in the hoodie. Instead, he has responded with just one line, "Call me asap.".

I hurriedly open my contacts and select Ares.

"Morgen, that was quick."

"Yeah. What's up Ares? You know that woman?"

"We both do, I'm sure. I can't remember her name, but I know I have seen her walking the streets of Minwall. I've been looking through our records for prostitution or drug arrests over the last year, but no luck so far."

The realization hits me like a truck. She is a sex worker from Minwall. Detective Ares is right…I have spoken to her before, I know it. Why can't I remember her name? I have only been out of Minwall for a few months… have I already forgotten everything from the eight years of dealing with the city regulars?

"Ares, you're a genius. I have dealt with her before…but it feels like it was a while ago."

"You haven't been gone that long Morgen." Detective Ares laughs.

"Sometimes it feels like forever, sometimes it's like I'm still right there."

"I wish you still were. But I'm glad you got out when you did, you know it never gets better here."

This is something everyone in Minwall Police Department understands intimately. It is a topic that is talked to death among cops, but so few of them actually try to do anything about it. Unfortunately for Ares, I have zero interest in joining this conversation today.

"Ares, I'm sending you another picture right now. Do you recognize the other woman in this photo?"

I hear the ping of Ares' email; he must be sitting at his desk right now. There are a few moments of silence before Ares speaks again.

"Morgen...where the fuck did you get this photo?"

I am surprised by the phrasing of his question...cops cuss more than anyone I know, but he sounds desperate, almost accusatory. I am immediately reminded of the minor arrestable offenses I committed to get these pictures. Offenses that occurred outside of Detective Ares' jurisdiction...meaning not his problem.

"I found a trail camera on a property near Binkin Trail. I was looking through the pictures and felt like someone was watching me, so I stole the SD card. These were the only photos that weren't deer."

"The second woman in these photos...she was just reported missing this morning."

Chapter Forty-Four: Julia Preston

As promised, when I open my eyes the next morning, Elaine is sleeping in the bed across the room. The gray fleece blanket wrapped tightly around her small frame, fuzzy hairs sticking up from the chocolate-colored braid hanging down her back. I lay completely still, focusing on each breath going in and out. How could I have been so naïve to think that the old man is good to us…that there is no price to pay for us leaving our cages? Without even realizing it, I have let Elaine pay that price. How could I let Elaine pay that price? What is he doing to her?

She looks so peaceful and small, her shoulders slowly rising and falling in tune with her breathing. I have never had to imagine the things that have been Elaine's reality every day of her life. Suddenly, I feel so responsible for everything that is happening here. I have let myself break to avoid feeling pain. I have remained meek and obedient to a man who is holding me hostage, letting myself actually believe there is goodness in him. Goodness that I have brought out, that has earned me something more than a life in a cage. *The cage.* There are still women in cages living without any light or food or hope. What is he doing to those women that he has spared me of? Why am I being spared?

It feels like hours going by while I lay here, unable to move. I need answers. The stillness of the house is suddenly broken by a muffled scream of terror. I sit up, clutching my blanket, an immediate chill spreading down my spine. Elaine doesn't stir at all, her breathing still heavy with deep sleep. I stare at the door, wondering if I imagined the whole thing. Slowly, careful to be as silent as possible, I creep towards the door, pressing my hands against the thick wood. I gently press my ear against the grain, feeling the uneven groves on my delicate cartilage.

I can hear a man talking…the old man. What is he saying? It's almost a low growl…I can't make out the words, but somehow the mere sound of it has fear pumping through my veins. I have never heard him like this. The responding noises are absolutely heartbreaking. A muffled whining, begging, pleading. A woman's voice. Does he have one of the caged girls upstairs? He must…there's no way anyone else would be in this house…only prisoners in this prison…and one jailer.

"Please! Please! I'll do anything…please don't kill me."

A deep, wicked laugh. He is enjoying this. She is terrified and he is enjoying this.

I cover my mouth with my hand. I want to scream. He is hurting a woman out there. This is the old man that has been in front of my face the whole time and I never saw him like this. I never saw him for what he really is…a monster.

I am pressed against the door so hard; the side of my face is beginning to hurt. Ignoring the pain, I keep pressing, hoping to hear every little sound…wanting to be a fly on the wall, if only to sear her face into my mind before she is never seen again. The creak of a drawer and metallic clanging.

"Nooooooo! No! No! No! Please!" A desperate, sobbing plea followed by a gurgling sound.

A muffled blood curdling scream sends chills down my arms, gagging, stifled words I could not make out.

Clanging, clattering, I pray she is fighting but I instantly understand there is no winning this match.

My fingernails clutch the door, cracking under the pressure, I want to scream. I want to help this faceless, nameless girl that I share so much with. *The sound of chair legs thudding against the floor, scraping and squealing.* My fingers digging deep in the door, wooden splinters entering my skin. It feels like I am in this moment for a lifetime. *A yelp of pain, gagging, choking, gurgling.* Silence.

The old man laughed, and she spoke no more.

I drop my ear from the door, knowing it is over now. I allow my body to slide to the floor, feeling small and defeated. How many girls have died since I have been here? I have been so focused on doing anything to live…I never considered how many haven't.

No longer caring about staying silent, I stomp to Elaine's bed and stare down at her hunched little form. Still sleeping soundly. Like a woman's last breath didn't just happen in the next room, at the hands of the monster holding us captive. I drop to my knees and shake Elaine. She murmurs, fighting her own consciousness, choosing to remain asleep. I grab both shoulders and shake her so violently the bed begins to wobble, a loud thud emitting in a steady rhythm each time the bed frame hits the wall. Her eye lids fly open, revealing more red than white surrounding the amber irises. The bags under her eyes appeared more pronounced, whether from a lack of sleep or tears, I wasn't sure.

"Jules, what is going on?"

"He just killed a girl. In the kitchen. I could hear it."

"Jules, go to sleep."

169

Elaine turns, facing the wall and closing her eyes again. I stare at the back of her head, jaw gaping, unable to comprehend how she could be so cold. She must misunderstand me...or think she is dreaming. I twist her body to face me again and she sighs loudly, eyes springing open once again.

"Elaine, did you not hear me? The old man just killed a girl."

"I hear you just fine. What exactly do you think we are doing here, Julia? Do you think this is some vacation getaway where you meet new friends that become family and test your limits, only to discover you are stronger than you ever imagined and come out a whole new better version of you? We were abducted, Julia. He pays some guy to get him new girls, plays with them until he is bored, then kills them."

She is so matter of fact. No sadness or fear.

"Then why are we different? Why has he spared us?"

"He doesn't think you are ready to know everything yet. You will have your answers eventually, Jules. Please, just drop it and go back to sleep."

I sit dumbstruck at Elaine's answer. She is willing to let me be confused and scared, all because this monster doesn't think I am ready to know why I am worthy of being kept alive.

All at once I am so tired of letting this man control my world.

So tired of being okay with this life, it's like everything I felt when I first awoke in that cage is flooding back to me.

I won't die like this.

I have to fight.

"I need to know everything, now." The anger in my voice burning hot.

170

Elaine sits up, looking surprised to see an emotion in me that I have not shown inside of this place. She sighs heavily before responding.

"In all of the things I have done and that I am about to say…I need you to promise that you will not hate me. Promise that you will understand that all I have ever cared about is keeping you and me alive. Just you and me."

"I promise." I whisper, my heartbeat pounding swiftly in my ears so loudly I can barely hear my own words.

"I have been here a long time, Julia. A long time. I stopped trying to count the months long before you came. I had given up at first. Decided it was okay if I died…no one would even know the difference anyway. He liked that about me. He liked that I broke so easily. It probably fueled his ego, made him think he had that effect on me. The truth was, life had broken me long before I ever got snatched. You see, he likes fucking with girls psychologically before he physically destroys them. Most girls fight back. If he thinks he can't do his twisted brainwashing type bullshit on you, then he just gets rid of you. The game is done; you are no longer any fun. He wants the girls to love him…not because he earned it, but because he trained you to do it. We are just animals to him. He's a fucking pig. He feeds off the control. He kept me around because I let him believe that he was training me. Training me to love him, to be controlled by him…to work for him."

Elaine took a deep breath and sighed before continuing, "When you came into the cages, everything changed for me. You are the only person in my entire life that has ever treated me with love. You wanted nothing in return but my friendship and love. I have never felt that before…not even from my own family. I knew that I couldn't lose you…that it

171

would be worth living in this hell hole if it gave me one true friend in this life. I told the old man that I saw something in you. That if he spared you, I would make sure that you would work for him too."

Tears pool in my eyes as I whisper, "Elaine…what do you mean, work for him?"

Chapter Forty-Five: Riley Morgen

Detective Ares' discovery that another missing woman has been linked to Binkin Trail has brought some spark back into Minwall Police Department's investigation. His sergeant has allowed him to spilt his time between these missing cases and the homicide investigation of Meredith Stokes. A small spark is better than no flame at all, I guess.

According to Ares, the latest missing woman is a known sex worker named Amanda Hutchings. She resides in a run-down motel in Minwall with her boyfriend, Theo. Theo came into Minwall Police Department to report Amanda missing after she never returned home four nights ago. She had been walking the streets, looking for a John, to make money to fuel their drug habit. According to Theo, this is very typical of them, and he had no reason to believe anything was wrong until he woke up at noon the next day and Amanda was not in the motel room. He waited a day to report her missing, thinking that maybe she got caught up somewhere and would be home soon. The two of them have lived together in that motel for six months, and he had no reason to believe that she would leave him without saying anything.

Detective Ares admitted to me that he had only glanced at the file when it came onto another detective's desk, and assumed that Amanda probably found some drugs, was on a binge, and was staying with someone else for a few days. He assumed this was a case that she left of her own accord and would be home within a few days, like the majority of missing persons reports. It wasn't until seeing the trail cam photos that he had any reason to believe anything was suspicious.

While I am not technically employed by any police department anymore, in Detective Ares' eyes, I am the lead on this investigation. I think I just have the privilege of location in this case. Ares has been spending any available time talking to people who live on the streets, specifically sex workers and known drug users in the area of the Minwall motel that Amanda was living in. He is hoping to track Amanda's last movements, and ideally get a license plate for the last car she was seen getting in. He has been showing the picture of the woman in a hoodie around also, but so far no one has identified her. It has been a slow process at this point…mostly because the people he stops aren't exactly keen to talk to the police.

While Ares works the area of Minwall for any leads, I have taken to spending my nights sitting in the woods near Binkin Trail. Not exactly the ideal stake out situation, but probably my best option for any results. So far, there has been nothing but deer walking by and animal noises in the distance that make my skin crawl. There is something so anxiety inducing about being alone and having to question just how alone you really are. I love nature but there is something entirely too creepy about sitting completely still, in the dark, trespassing on someone else's property, in a thickly wooded area, waiting for a possible suspect in a woman's disappearance. Every sound makes my skin prickle and breathing quicken…and there are plenty of sounds. I have never felt more like a city girl than during these stake outs.

So here I sit, crouched against a tree trunk on Sean Hitchcock's property wishing I had any other lead than one that left me hiding alone in the woods at night. I am surprisingly comfortable with the idea of trespassing on this stranger's property at this point…it's starting to feel like a home away from home. At least that's what I repeat to myself every time I hear a noise that convinces me I may find Bigfoot out here before I find any actual suspects.

I have no idea what time it is, for fear of turning on the light on my watch and being spotted from a mile away. It has been hours since I have moved from my spot, convinced that it gives me the perfect view of a makeshift path lit by the moonlight. I shiver slightly, dealing with the nightly temperature drop that has started to come with fall around the corner. I should have brought a jacket, or a hoodie.

I still, my blood suddenly hot and pounding. Did I just see movement? My eyes dart around, hoping to locate the source of movement and avoid being caught off guard by anything…or anyone. A twig snaps so loudly, I jump. As if my eyes and ears are suddenly able to work in unison, a figure comes into my view. Human. Walking cautiously, head down watching the ground as if fearful of tripping over some unseen object. My body is desperate to move; begging to jump up and confront the person I have been waiting days for. I refuse to give in to that impulse. I breathe light, soft breaths. I still every part of my body consciously, praying the darkness has made me one with this tree trunk I have grown to know so well. *Go into the moonlight. Go into the moonlight.* As if I will it to happen, the figure steps into the pathway of moonlight and I nearly yelp with excitement at the black hoodie she is wearing. *It is her.*

I can't believe my luck. It is her, walking nearly the same path the trail cam witnessed. I am hoping to give her enough of a lead that I can follow her unnoticed. It will be hard in these conditions, between the sticks and fallen leaves, sound is likely to give someone away before sight would. I can only hope that some distance and the darkness will be my friends in this endeavor. I let my patience guide me, which is probably the hardest feat I have ever done. Pure adrenaline is begging my body to act. Finally, it is my time to slowly stand, carefully choosing each footstep to avoid any noise. I try to match her steps, hoping to blend the noise together. The path feels never ending. The sound of my heartbeat is pounding in my ears as I put so much effort into every single foot fall. She has heard nothing, never looking back, only down at her own foot work.

We are nearing Binkin Trail. Her steps become more rushed, less calculated. Has she heard me behind her or has the thinning of the forest just made her steps easier? All at once, she turns and leaves the wood line, stepping into the open air of Binkin Trail. She is now bathed in moonlight, walking toward the dirt trail path, seeming to choose the easier path to walk. I remain in the shadows of the wood line for as long as possible, realizing that I am running out of options. I will have to step into the open soon, and risk being seen. At least the ground will be much quieter on the trail.

I pause, judging the distance between us and give into the only option I can. I step out of the privacy of the trees and walk towards the dirt trail. I can see her ahead of me, going right on a bend in the trail. I sped up my steps only slightly, not wanting to lose a visual, and hoping to find a section of the bend I can watch from while I allow her to regain distance. I round the corner and nearly scream as she steps out from a shadowed portion of the bend. She lifts her head, an

176

unflinching stillness consuming her features. Our eyes meet, with a flicker of recognition between us.

"Officer Morgen?"

It all comes crashing back to me. Her face. Her story. Her name.

"Elaine?"

Before I can say anything else, Elaine turns and sprints into the forest. Still fighting shock, I give chase, all the while seeing nothing but the trees.

She is gone.

Chapter Forty-Six: Him

I have an itch underneath my skin that I just cannot scratch. It is hidden much deeper than the layers of epidermis accessible to me. I didn't expect it to come so soon after the skinless whore, but there is a sense of tension around me right now that is bringing out a certain version of me, I typically suppress. I can do without the old bastard's business, but I haven't heard from him in months. I know him well enough to know he needs a new girl every month or so, at least…if not sooner. He has been a steady source of income for as many years as I have been in business. That was part of our deal. I have steady income and free rein, and he has my silence and access to an endless supply of my product. I assumed he was laying low…smart enough to know that eyes are on Bearpoint right now. Smart enough to know that these things come in waves…people pretend to care about some girl gone missing, but eventually forget she ever existed. Then business goes on as usual.

Everything was fine.

Everything was riding the expected wave that comes from a higher quality product. So, tell me why is my brother involving himself with that fucking pig? What exactly does he think he is doing questioning me and my business? Why is he talking to Riley fucking Morgen?

I want them both dead.

I might just have to let my brother meet the side of me that he seems to have so many questions about. There's one I can finally let my dad have a front row seat to. He'll bring the popcorn, spending the whole time laughing, feeling like his life is finally complete, I'm sure. A real dream come true for him. The day he finally has only one son.

It is one thing for him to question me himself...he's been doing that my whole life. He's too stupid to actually figure anything out on his own. But for him to start fueling suspicion from other people...thinking he can destroy everything I have built.

I will end him.

I find myself driving to Minwall, I need the relief, I need this itch to stop so I can think clearly. I loathe this feeling...*I will not lose control.* The forty-minute drive is usually relaxing, usually lightly exciting knowing that I have a bit of fun ahead of me, typically empty of any other cars or human beings for most of the way. I grip the steering wheel with knuckles void of their usual color, feeling the rage clawing its way up my throat. A lion's fury bursting through me, I yell into the void of my car, causing the windows to shake at the sound.

A deep inhale. A deep exhale. The illusion of control is necessary right now. Even if I want to rip my own skin off piece by piece until I find the source of this itch. Soon enough, I will have someone else to rip apart, and that soothes me in some small way. I take my time finding the right one, to rush is to make mistakes. I do not lose control. I do not make mistakes. I wait for the right one. The solo gazelle, weak, unloved by even themselves, searching for a fix so desperately that nothing could sound unreasonable if it ultimately led to soothing their sickness. Unaware of my desperate need to soothe my own.

179

I stalk the blocks surrounding the motels that no one but my ideal target would inhabit. These blocks are full of the forgotten. Not worth the city's money for cameras, not worth police time to pick up addicts and prostitutes. A literal hunting ground of gazelles, unsuspecting of a lion.

There she is.

Number 244.

A small woman, slightly dirty, slightly unsteady on her feet. No one else in sight.

I pull my vehicle over to the side of the road and roll down my passenger window.

She speaks first, "You lookin' for a date?"

"I am. Get in."

Chapter Forty-Seven: Riley Morgen

I lay awake in my bed, staring at the ceiling, waiting to hear the ping of a new text message on my phone. I texted Detective Ares as I walked home from Binkin Trail, after discovering the woman in the hoodie is Elaine. I can't believe I didn't recognize her right away in the photo. I have spoken to Elaine many times while on patrol in Minwall. As an officer, you interact with so many different walks of life every single day. Some, you know will remain stuck in the life their choices have led them to. Some, you see that hope that they will one day believe in themselves enough to turn things around. Elaine was someone I had hope in.

Elaine had been a sex worker in Minwall for longer than I had policed there. In a city like Minwall, officers don't spend their time arresting sex workers unless they have an ulterior motive behind it. They know the woman has information they need, but would only give it up to get a deal on a charge of their own. I had a different approach when it came to the women who had found themselves in this place. Sex workers typically don't just happen. Most women don't just wake up one day and decide on a career path that includes living on the street, getting in the car with strange men and selling their bodies for sometimes less than hourly wage. These are women who have gone through terrible things, and many times had been forced into a life they never signed up for. These are women who deserve my respect and concern. And from a cop's perspective…these are women who know everything that goes on and everyone that is around.

My relationship with Elaine started with simple acts of kindness that I would have done for any woman on hard times, honestly. I saw her walking the same blocks every night, many times looking high, never looking clean. I stopped out with her and introduced myself, not to be a cop, but to be a human being. I gave her water, would get her a cheeseburger from the drive thru when I went. Small, simple acts that build trust between two people who are so far apart, they need a bridge built between them. I would not call us friends. I don't think Elaine every truly believed that I did not have any ulterior motive, and I didn't blame her for that. From what I did know about her; life had taught her not to trust anyone.

We were not friends, but I did care about her. From one human to another, I wanted her to be okay. Nearly two years ago, I left the precinct normally and stopped at the drive thru to grab some extra food for the women I knew I would see that night. I never saw Elaine that night. It was unusual, but not unheard of. I assumed she was using somewhere…or in the car with some John. One night led to another, then another. I never saw Elaine again. I always wondered what had happened to her, always hoping that she had moved on to another area…that I wouldn't end up responding to her dead body in some alleyway.

The last thing I ever expected was to see her in Bearpoint…all this time later.

Why would she be wandering around in the woods in the middle of the night, in the middle of a nowhere town like Bearpoint? She certainly isn't doing business out here, is she?

Maybe she found some John who wanted to wife her up. But then why would she be leading Amanda into the woods, then Amanda is reported missing by her boyfriend a day later? Suddenly I see Elaine's face in my head again. The surprise in her eyes, features hardened since the last time I saw her. She was always thin, though her face seemed even more hallowed out than before. Somehow, her eyes were clearer than I had ever seen them. Maybe she is clean now...maybe she truly started a new life out here with some family I didn't know about. I could let that thought calm me, bring me some form of peace in all of this...if it weren't for Amanda.

Is Elaine involved in these women that have gone missing?

The sun shines through my bedroom window, nearly blinding in its intrusion, but the warmth on my skin is welcoming. When was the last time I actually slept? It has been a few days since I had gotten anything more than a short nap, for sure. I have gotten used to very little sleep after working in law enforcement, so despite my lack of it, I am not even tired. My mind is buzzing with questions.

The sound of my phone ringing causes me to jump, suddenly pulled from the swirling questions drowning my brain.

"Good morning, Ares. You got my text?"

"I did...I don't understand what Elaine would be doing in Bearpoint. I looked into her criminal history before calling; she has been tied to the area of Minwall for her entire life. She went to high school here...Minwall Police Department had responded to her childhood home numerous times, apparently her parents were not winning any parent of the year awards either. Twenty months ago, all contacts with her and officers stop completely. It's strange because nearly every other night, at least one officer had field contact with Elaine. They were just a quick summary of seeing her in a certain area, what she was seen wearing that night, some basic conversation...nothing remarkable. But the contacts were consistent. What I find so interesting is that it suddenly just stopped after being consistent for so long."

"Well, it's possible that is when she came out here to Bearpoint. Did you find any ties to known associates out here?"

"None at all. As far as I can find, her father has been in prison since she was in middle school. Her mother died of an overdose when she was in tenth grade. She had no siblings. In her interactions with police, she is always alone. A few times she was caught with a John, but there is no record of any friends or associates. Doesn't mean they don't exist...but they don't according to our records."

"Do you think she is actually missing, but was never reported?"

"I considered the same thing, Morgen. But I mean, she ran from you. That doesn't really scream a victim in need of help."

"True. I just can't shake the feeling that this is all connected."

"It's possible she is involved from an offender side of these cases, Morgen."

"It's possible. I just don't think that fits her criminal history. It seems like quite a jump to go from a victim in domestic violence and a long-time sex worker to abducting and killing women."

"I agree. There are pieces we just aren't seeing yet. I will keep digging."

184

I hang up with Detective Ares still thinking about everything he said. Elaine spent her life in Minwall...and there is no proof that she would have had the means or desire to suddenly just start over in a new town. If she was a victim, or totally innocent, why would she have run from me in the woods? Why is she walking the woods near Binkin Trail in the middle of the night in the first place? And even if she has no connection to Julia Preston, or Meredith Stokes, what is the connection between Elaine and Amanda Hutchings? Even with a brain full of questions and zero answers, it is clear that something is going on in Bearpoint and I am going to figure out what it is.

Chapter Forty-Eight: Julia Preston

I stare at Elaine, the silence between us thick, desperate for an answer and terrified at her coming words.

"Jules, this is the part you will hate me for."

I want to soothe Elaine; I can see the pain she is carrying. I want to promise her I will never hate her, and keep that promise. Something in me stops me from saying the words out loud. I feel like I have no words left. I am desperate for her words, and terrified for each one at the same time. I grab Elaine's hands and hold them tightly, lightly stroking my thumb up and down, hoping to convey everything I wish I was brave enough to say in that simple gesture.

Elaine looks down at our interlocked hands and continues, "Do you remember how you got here?"

Her question surprises me. I nod and finally speak, "I was grabbed off the street near my apartment. I went out for a run, but never made it to the park. I don't remember much after he grabbed me, I think I was drugged or something. I remember being dragged to a car. I remember his face looking at me from the front seat, I was tied up in the back. Then I woke up in the cage...here."

"So, you do remember that the old man didn't abduct you?"

"Yeah. He looked like he was closer to my age...maybe late twenties. He was good looking...I will never forget his face...it's burned in my memory."

186

"The old man pays him to abduct women for him. I don't know the full extent of that fucked up relationship. All I know is that the old man wants to have his own way of getting women here...for free. He kept me alive because I can convince women to come here. Prostitutes. Addicts. The type of women that I have spent my life around...the type of woman I was before I came here. I know what to say to get them here."

I feel bile rising in my throat. My head is spinning, immediately woozy, chest tightening, pain surging with every breath. I must have misheard her. I must be misunderstanding what Elaine is saying. She can't be a part of this. She can't be bringing women into this hell. How can she love one victim so much and be heartless enough to bring another to slaughter?

She must see the shock on my face, the pale of my skin. Maybe she just doesn't want to give me a chance to respond because she continues speaking again.

"At first, I was doing it to make him trust me...I knew once he did, he would let me leave to get a girl and I could escape. I just wanted to escape and never think of this place again. Then you came. I knew I couldn't leave you here alone to die. I told you to break so he wouldn't kill you just for the fun of it...just to avoid dealing with the extra hassle of the fight. Then it came to me. If I convinced the old man that you could get a different quality of woman than I could...I could keep you alive...I could give you worth in his eyes. If I could convince him that you and I would do this...then eventually, we would be able to escape. Together."

"How could you let other women die?" I whisper, fighting down the hard knot in my throat.

187

"They would do the same thing if they could save themselves. I can't care about everyone in this world, Jules. All that matters to me is to get us out alive."

There it is...the fundamental difference between Elaine and I. Elaine was molded by a world that taught her to trust no one. A world that has a sole goal of survival...by any means necessary. A world that taught her that it is better them than her. A deep sadness washes over me at this realization. Elaine has done terrible things, with the goal of saving me. If not for her convincing the old man...I would probably be dead already. How can I hate someone for doing what they believe is the only way out? She could have escaped already and never thought about me again...but she didn't. She came back to our prison, for the sole reason of protecting me. Who am I to judge what a human being does to survive? I owe everything to Elaine...there can be no judgement in this situation.

I again try to swallow down the hard lump that has formed in my throat. The only way I can help us all...is to get out of this cabin.

"What do I have to do?"

Chapter Forty-Nine: Riley Morgen

I wake with a start and find myself slumped over on the living room couch, notebook on my lap and pen still clutched in my hand. When did I fall asleep? I jump as I hear a loud knock at the front door. I suddenly realize why I woke up and walk to the window, peering out to see who is the knocker that has disturbed my sleep. My mother. I rub the sleep from my eyes and unlock the door, just as she begins loudly calling my name.

"Hello Mom." I stand back, holding the door open for her to come inside. She walks past me swiftly, setting her purse on my kitchen table and staring at the piles of paperwork scattered about.

"Riley Rose, what is all this?"

"It's just paperwork for a case I'm helping my friend at Minwall PD with."

She is staring at each paper, drinking in any information she can. "But you're not a cop anymore. Why are you helping with some investigation?" She then turns to look at me for the first time since her uninvited intrusion and speaks again, "Look at you, when is the last time you slept?"

"Well actually, you just woke me up. I'm helping because the detective is my friend, it's not a big deal, Mom." The last thing I plan on doing right now is telling my mother that after finding evidence of a missing woman, I have dedicated all my free brain space to this investigation. I know it's not exactly a healthy way to mentally decompress from a trauma filled law enforcement career, but here I am.

My mom laughs, a fully overdramatized show of it, her head whipping backwards, hand on her belly. "Nothing has ever been 'not a big deal' with you, Riley Rose. Even after leaving your career, you are still letting it take over your life! Just admit that this is what you are meant to do with your life and go do it. At least make 'em pay you for it."

"It's not that simple, Mom. Even though I miss it sometimes, I can't bring myself to deal with everything it entails anymore. If I could work for myself as a cop, I would."

"So, get a private investigator's license."

She says it so simply, as if it should have just been obvious to me. I had never considered that there is a way for me to still enjoy the investigation aspect of law enforcement, while working for myself.

"I haven't really put any thought into it…maybe I will be a PI eventually."

"You haven't put any thought into it because you're too busy working for free for Minwall Police Department. Have you gone to therapy yet?"

"No, Mom." I roll my eyes, beyond tired of hearing the same probing questions. When will she get tired of asking them?

"Look at yourself Riley. Seriously. You have to actually work at getting back to a good place. I'm glad you are away from such a toxic environment but problems don't just fix themselves. I'm your mother, I know you are not okay right now. Please, just listen to me and start doing the work."

I sigh. Why do things sound more annoying coming from my mother? I know she is right, I know it is coming from a loving place, but I can't fight that sometimes it feels so invasive. I am just too old for my mom to be weighing in on every one of my life decisions. Between my exhaustion and this same argument currently beating at my spirit, I feel defeated. I simply respond, "I know...I will."

Thankfully, the discussion finishes with my half assed agreement.

"How about I take you out to lunch like old times? Let's go to the city and spend the day together."

I happily agree, feeling almost excited to get out of the house and hopefully get my head away from the investigation of Julia Preston...if only for a few hours.

****

When I return home, I feel that some of the weight of the last few days has dissipated and my head feels a bit clearer. Whether it is from the big lunch, or from allowing my mind to escape for a few hours, the exhaustion of barely sleeping in days is finally catching up with me. I am worn out. All I want is a hot shower, a fuzzy pair of socks and a long sleep in the comfort of my cozy bed.

I drop my purse on the kitchen table, feeling slightly foggy, and head for the shower. I stop dead in my tracks; eyes locked on the open bathroom window that has come into my view. There is no way I left the bathroom window open. I have never opened the bathroom window before...why is it open? Would my mom have opened the bathroom window before we left? I turn and quietly walk to my purse, grabbing my firearm, and begin clearing my own house. The cabin is small, just by entering the home, I can see that no one is in the living room or kitchen. I quickly check the bathroom, then make my way to the only other room in the cabin...my bedroom.

I check the bedroom and closet, even under the bed. The bedroom is clear. As I lift myself from the floor, thankful no one is hiding under the bed, I see an envelope laying on the quilt of my bed. I feel my heart stop, my skin prickling with dread, veins surging with blood so fast it must be trying to restart my no longer beating heart. My head is spinning, whether with exhaustion, shock, or from the sudden rush of lifting myself off the floor, I don't know. Probably a combination of all three. There is an envelope on my bed. Someone was in my house.

I grab the envelope and rush out of my bedroom to shut the bathroom window. I make sure it is locked. Did I check that it was locked before? I can't remember. I rip open the envelope, desperate to see what this creep is going to say this time. Again, it is a typed one-line letter. This time, the words bring bile to my throat.

"Do you want to be the next girl on the news? Maybe you'll be home for my next visit.
P.S. Julia is dead. Don't let yourself be next."

I drop the letter and take off running, leaving through the front door and running through the forest to the right of my house. The forest that leads to the only neighbor close enough to my house to give me answers. I am no one's prey...and I am sick of the lack of answers. I step carefully through the tall grass of the unloved yard belonging to my neighbor. It is clear the maintenance of this house has been nonexistent for quite some time. I gingerly step on the front porch, choosing each step with consideration, hoping I won't fall through the warped and rotten boards.

I pound my fist against the front door, a police style knock that probably came off a bit more aggressive than intended. I take a deep breath, trying to relax myself and release the anger that threatens to boil over at this undeserving elderly man. I can hear the creaking and whining of floor boards inside the house, straining from the weight of someone walking toward the front door. I give the man extra time before knocking again, assuming it probably takes him a bit longer to get to the door than it would a younger man.

The door groans as it partially opens, revealing the face that I have seen watching me from the window numerous times.

A gruff voice escapes from the darkness, "What do you want?"

It takes me a second to recover from the brashness of the question. I again take a deep breath, and muster up the friendliness of a neighbor that I'm hoping doesn't sound as fake as it feels coming from me. "Hello! My name is Riley; I am your neighbor, over there." I point towards my home, smiling calmly.

"What do you want?"

Okay. Clearly, my feigned friendliness is pointless here. I decide to get right to the point. "Someone broke into my home today and I am wondering if you saw anything unusual from about eleven this morning to four this afternoon?"

The man shifts on his feet, not necessarily uncomfortable with the question, instead seeming uncomfortable with the burden of standing.

I worry I am putting unnecessary burden on this man and shift my tone momentarily, "Are you okay? I can come in for a minute if you need to sit down."

His response is swift, "No. I am fine."

"Okay, sorry, I didn't mean to intrude. I am just hoping to get any information you may have."

The man looked me up and down for a few long moments, silently questioning if he can trust me, his mouth moving slightly as if chewing on the inside of his cheek. I wait patiently, trying to appear unthreatening to this man who probably hasn't had much human interaction in a long time.

He speaks suddenly, his gravelly voice deep and dark eyes piercing into mine, "There was a man walking through the back of my property today."

Excitement burns in my chest, "About what time did you see him?"

"Close to eleven, I guess. I saw that red car driving down the road. I sat in my chair in the living room...then saw movement out the back window."

The red car...he must mean my mom's car. The man who broke in...he must have been watching me. Watching my mom. I feel a deep pit of sickness turning and bubbling in my stomach. I swallow a hard bubble forming in the back of my throat before continuing, "What did he look like?"

The man squints, his face scrunching slightly, seemingly pulling the memory from the depths of his mind. "I didn't see his face...just a dark t-shirt and green sweatpants."

I thank my neighbor and head back to my house, convinced that I must have been watched this morning. How often is this man waiting in the woods near my house? I feel so violated knowing that I am being treated as this man's prey. As I walk, I think about the description the elderly man gave…dark t-shirt and green sweatpants. Could this be the same man I saw in the dark green joggers the day I found Julia Preston's locket?

Chapter Fifty: Him

As I drive from the area, the hooker tells me of a couple close by locations that we can have some privacy. I let her talk as we keep driving.

"Where are we going? I just told you to take that right. Turn around."

I muster all the control I can and ignore my itching skin, burning me all over, begging me to slice this bitch up right here at this red light. I rub my forehead, and exhale deeply, attempting to convey a sense of awkwardness before speaking. Let her believe I am not an experienced John.

"I have a weird request."

"That will cost you extra."

"No, no. I mean. My parents are coming into town tomorrow morning and they think I have a serious girlfriend. They just wouldn't understand that I'm...I'm not interested in women. I need you to...you know, just pretend to be my girlfriend. Just to get them off my back, you know."

Her face softens ever so slightly. I am in. I am just a bank account that has no interest in getting my rocks off. I am the easiest money she is going to make all night...and I'm going to let her name her price. Sure, I could just drug her right now. Tie her up and leave her in the trunk. I could beat her unconscious and save the drugs for someone worth keeping alive. But there is something so satisfying about full control. I can control her mind, body and soul...she is mine completely.

196

Mine to end, however I wish. I feel the itch screaming under my skin, the excitement bubbling hot and quick.

"I can do that honey but it's not gunna be cheap. You are taking up a lot of my precious time."

I nearly laugh. Nothing about this skank is precious. She must really believe I am an idiot.

"I'll pay whatever I need to."

****

As we pull up to my property, I take the first driveway, which leads to the old barn buildings further back on the property. My excitement is nearly boiling over, but I'm honestly just thankful to get out of this car and stop listening to this waste of functioning organs give herself a fake backstory to tell my nonexistent parents. This ride has tested my patience, but I am finally home. I am finally in my domain, where I can take off my muzzle, my mask, so to speak.

I park in front of the middle barn and let her know that I just need to make sure I locked up the animals for the night before we head up to the house. She offers to help, and I agree. Silly skank. You have made this so easy. I unlock the padlock and hold the barn door open for her. *Such a gentleman.*

"Where are the animals?"

"Right here."

She turns around and looks me right in the eyes. That flicker of fear as the realization hits is so delicious. *Yes, I am the only animal here.*

I grab her by the throat, lifting her off her feet. She clutches my hands, gagging, legs kicking, struggling for air and the stability of the ground beneath her dangling feet. I squeeze

197

until I see the petechiae forming in the whites of her shit brown eyes. Not so soon. Not like this. A few minutes of release is nowhere near enough for me in this moment. I loosen my grip on her throat, dropping her to the dirt of the barn floor. She clutches her throat protectively, gasping for air, wheezing, eyes bulging.

In one swift motion, I am upon her again, grabbing her jaw and forcing her head backwards. The control I exhibit in the snap of her head is impressive. Don't break her neck. Not yet. Control yourself and enjoy this. Deep inhale, deep exhale.

I pull the hawkbill knife from my pocket and flip it open, staring down at the wretched, pathetic face beneath me. The begging faintly registering behind the excitement pounding loudly in my ears. She balls up her fists, swings wildly, striking me in the legs a number of times. Doesn't she know I don't feel pain? I don't feel anything, silly skank. We are both outside of our bodies right now, in our own ways.

In one swift motion, without a second thought or a single change in my expression, I slam the knife into her left eye, wrenching it sideways before pulling it out. The scream leaving her worn out mouth reverberates from the old wood walls. It enters my ears, gliding through me, meeting my soul, surging around via my bloodstream like little fingers scratching away at my insides. The relief is intensely sensual. The prickling sensation dances up my back and I feel alive again.

It all comes flooding into my mind, every annoyance that brought me to this place. Riley Morgen coming into my domain and thinking she can poke around, looking for answers where she doesn't belong. My brother, my twin, who should be standing beside me in all things, betraying the

198

deepest part of my core, our family legacy. That old fucking bastard, making me question our business deals…the deal that has kept everything running smoothly for the last fifteen years.

There is no more need for control. I am in my empire. In these unassuming wood walls, I am God.

I slam the knife into her soft warm flesh, over and over again. Again, and again. Unleashing every bit of anger that has plagued my peace. Each pull back of the knife splattering whore blood onto her God's face. It is so undeserving of such a remarkable end. The taste metallic and rich. The smell of iron and fear filling my nostrils, I snort it greedily, savoring each molecule of scent.

I grab her scalp, lifting her head and drive the knife nearly straight through the neck. I hack angrily, blood pooling the floor and covering my entire hand until my flesh cannot be seen. A swift, violent motion and the snap of the neck bones boom in my ears and immediately releases the anger pulsing in my veins. Her body drops and her head remains dangling from my hand.

I stand, breathing heavily, and sigh. The itch is gone. The relief is so deep, I feel that I could sleep for days. I am the addict who just expelled the syringe into my veins and it feels so fucking good. I roll my neck, appreciating the irony of the cracking sound in my ears.

"Ah, that's better."

I am renewed.

Number 244.

I walk outside, still carrying a decapitated head, walking past the third barn, towards the burn pit. I am not a fan of the smell of burning flesh. It's quite unpleasant, actually. But hey,

I'm suddenly in a very good mood. I want to throw my dad a bone, have some bonding time. I toss the head into the burn pit and go back to the barn to do the same for the body.

After rearranging everything for a perfect bonfire, I head back to the house to get my dad. He is going to love this...I am such a good son. No wonder I am the favorite.

Chapter Fifty-One: Julia Preston

The base need humans have to survive will make you do things that your moral compass never thought you were capable of doing. I can't get past the feeling that I have a moral obligation to save every woman that enters this hell. I hate that this is the position I am in. I have to believe that if I can walk out of this cabin, with the old man believing that I will be bringing home another woman for him to murder, then I can get help. Not just escape, but get help that will save every woman in here. I have to do everything possible to make the old man trust me...to believe that I have truly broken to his will.

I will do anything I need to do for this small hope that now feels within my reach. I have to hold on to what is left of me...while putting on the greatest act I will ever have to perform in my life. I know the old man believes that I have broken. I know it because I am alive. I am in a bedroom with Elaine instead of hunched inside of a dog cage, praying my captor will chain me to a chair upstairs and stick candies into my mouth. I know he believes that I have broken...and I think in some ways I believe that I have too. Those are the moments that I remind myself I am doing this for Elaine, and for each of the girls in those cages.

Elaine explained to me that the old man is doing this so that we can bring home new girls for him. Girls for him to torture, rape, beat, starve and eventually kill. He does not want to work with the man that is bringing him girls anymore. I wonder how they are connected. I thought they could be related, but they do not share any features that I can remember. I assume the old man still works, or maybe has another family, because he leaves the cabin for many hours at a time consistently. I don't think he sleeps here. Living in the upstairs has allowed me to start to notice patterns, notice the front door opening and closing, the sound of a car door, the voices of the caged women when they are brought upstairs…the rattling of their chains. For so long, I only knew the side of him that he showed to me when I was let out of the cage and chained to that chair. I can now hear what he does to the other women on their trips upstairs. He is a monster. This cabin, this murderous monster side of him…it can't be all there is. I'm convinced of one thing… I am witnessing his secret side, the life he hides from everyone else.

Chapter Fifty-Two: Riley Morgen

Knowing that I am being watched, being threatened in my own home like this has left me unsettled. I decided to go back to my notebook, eyes gliding over my suspect list again and again, deep in thought, not really seeing anything. I can't sit back waiting for answers when I am now being hunted in my own home. I have to go through each of these suspects and get them off the list until there is only one left.

At this point, the man in the green joggers is a strong suspect. I first saw him near the area that I found Julia Preston's locket. Now my neighbor gives me the same description for the man that possibly broke into my house, leaving a threatening letter. A letter that claims that Julia Preston is already dead. I need to identify him as quickly as possible. The only way to do that will be to stake out the areas I have seen him...just like I did with Elaine. I still have a ton of questions about why Elaine is here in Bearpoint...I just have no idea if she could be connected to Julia. Hopefully I will see her again during my surveillance for the man in the green joggers...two birds, one stone.

I can always go to The Conway to follow up with Jack. At least that's one person that I can easily track down. As far as Brady, he will likely be at the hardware store. I decide to delay that conversation, I already have the creeps about the latest letter in my bed...I really don't know that I need to put myself in a room with Brady right now. I'll put them off for the moment, but will eventually need to follow up with them so I can update this list.

The last two on the list are not exactly happy with me right now. Sheriff Marks doesn't want me anywhere near the sheriff's office. I don't mind obliging with that for the moment. I'd like to avoid a trespassing charge, and the anger that I know will come with conversating with that sorry excuse of a man. Deputy May is last on the list. I have been avoiding thinking about the entire May situation for the last few days, forcing myself to get lost in thoughts of Julia Preston instead. I feel guilty facing the truth that he is on this list. That *I* put him on this list. From a police mindset, I know that I am doing what I need to do…eliminate the people that could have possibly done this based on the evidence that I have been presented. As a friend, I feel like complete garbage. I betrayed the one person who has stuck their neck out for me, the one person that I should have had complete trust in this entire time. What an asshole, I am.

I think the best thing I can do right now is to eliminate Deputy May first. I need to do this, and I genuinely believe that I will be able to cross off his name then go crawling back to him begging him to forgive his asshole friend. It would be nice to have someone I can talk to here in Bearpoint again…especially since I have some creep breaking in my house and can't even report it since it could be Sheriff Marks or even Deputy May. Even if neither have anything to do with it, I won't let the sheriff feel justified in his telling me to mind my own business and let the men handle it. I roll my eyes just thinking about it.

Once I am decided that Deputy May needs to be investigated first, I realize there is no better time than the present. The sun will be setting soon, and I know that Deputy May works the day shift so he should be home with his brother, Jordan. I dress in a black hoodie and black pants, which seems to be the look everyone goes for in this town lately. The look of someone up to nefarious activities…I might as well join them. I jumble together a plan in my head while I get dressed, which means I don't really have a plan. I am going to walk the woods around May's property and hopefully see or hear something. Maybe I will see the green jogger or Elaine. It's a loose plan, but at least it's better than sitting at home listening for another possible break in.

****

The nights are getting colder in Bearpoint, unsure if the shivers I'm getting are from the chill in the air or the spooky sounds of the woods at night. Every tiny sound is magnified in the darkness, sensory deprivation doing its best to play tricks on me. I'm doing my best not to give into it. My mind keeps reminding me that I have now ran into two people out here at night, so I am doing my best to remain vigilant while watching where I step, as to prevent any extra sound. It feels like I have been walking for hours, the woods disorienting with the scenery looking so similar. It's as if I'm walking on an invisible treadmill hidden by the dirt and fallen leaves. Endlessly walking and getting nowhere at all.

Finally, I see a large cabin in the distance that I believe belongs to the Mays. At least I hope that I have calculated the walking distance correctly…otherwise I will be prowling on some stranger's property. Just like the green jogger. A shiver that definitely isn't from the chilly air runs through me. I

205

quickly glance at my watch, only willing to chance the glow for a brief moment. Just about ten o'clock. They should still be up so I will have to be careful.

I turn and head towards the cabin, stepping slow and gentle. Maybe this is stupid. Should I really be creeping up on a sheriff deputy's property at ten o'clock at night? Especially when he basically hates my guts. Well, it's stupid but I'm not turning back now. I have to find out everything I can on Derek May and I have to start somewhere. At least I remembered to bring my binoculars this time. Yet another random tool I acquired while working patrol.

I creep up as close as the tree cover will allow while still keeping me hidden. I pull out my binoculars and work on adjusting for a few moments. The cabin comes into view clearly and I slowly start to look around. It is a beautiful home. It looks much larger than the tiny log square that I now call mine. The outside appears completely normal and dull. Nothing of interest. I reposition myself until I am nearly aligned with a window. I nearly jump as I reposition the binoculars to my face and see two men in the living room of the home. For a brief second, I almost forgot they cannot see me, despite how clearly, I now see them.

Derek and Jordan May sit in the living room of their home, a small table between them, looking intense. They are big men, both in height and muscle, and it is obvious that they are identical. Even their mannerisms appear similar from my vantage point, both hunched, intensely staring at the table, one hand on their lips, tapping in thought. It is actually quite comical.

So odd that there would be two sets of identical twins living this close together, so similar in age, in such a small town. Maybe it's not. Maybe I am just looking for something suspicious in everything now. Whether from a complete lack of trust or a complete lack of sleep, I don't even know anymore. I attempt to readjust my binoculars again to see what they are looking at on the table. Some sort of paperwork. A laptop open between them as well. I recognize the Google logo in the upper left-hand corner, but can't make out any of the words on the screen.

With those two distracted, I decide to take a look around the property. There are multiple barns heading towards the back of the property, so I decide to start there. I walk the tree line for as long as I can until I have to walk into open grass. It really is a beautiful property. Even in the dark, I feel a sense of peace here.

I place my hand on the door of the first barn, pushing gently, trying to determine if the wood will creak and groan with any manipulation. I am stopped short of my goal, hand still raised towards the door, blood icy and thick in my veins as I hear the pump action racking of a shotgun behind me.

"Now hold it right there, little missy."

I am immediately shaking at the voice I do not recognize, deep, each word drawled out. I raise my hands and slowly begin to turn towards the voice. A flashlight is shining in my face, nothing but the barrel of a shotgun visible. *Oh crap, I am so stupid, I should not be here.*

The man shouts, "Derek! Jordan!"

I am so stupid. I should not be here. Why did I let myself do this?

Within a minute both Derek and Jordan are running across the lawn, toward the shotgun with a southern drawl.

Derek speaks first. "Dad, what is going...Riley?!?"

"You know this girl, Derek?"

"Yes, Dad, I know her." Even through my fear, I could hear a hint of disgust when he said it. He must still hate me. I don't blame him. I was already the asshole, now here I am trespassing on his property in the dark too. I might as well say goodbye to this friendship forever.

The shotgun lowers and I am suddenly greeted with a man who is clearly Mr. May. Even if I had not had this most embarrassing introduction, I would have known it from a mile away. His sons are his spitting image. A tall, broad-shouldered man, deep caramel skin slightly weathered with age, yet still handsome. His body hangs at an angle that makes me believe he is in pain...though not enough to be unable to sneak up on me, apparently. He smiles so warmly, like he didn't just come within an inch of ending my life and says, "Well hello there Miss Riley. You don't have to sneak around our property to see Derek, you can just come to the front door, you know."

I feel an immediate flush to my face and I am sure I am bright red, hoping that the darkness is acting as a cover to the changes in my face. "I am so sorry about that Mr. May. I'll get headed home now."

"Don't be silly, you're coming inside and meeting Derek's family properly."

I inwardly cringe at the awkward situation I have now forced Deputy May into. I send mental waves to him, hoping he suddenly has telepathy, *I am so sorry, you are officially allowed to ban me from your life forever after this.*

Once inside I am taken back by the beauty of the interior of this house. From the outside, it appears to be a typical log cabin, as my cabin is. The interior has been transformed, limiting the wood and instead using it only as accents. Huge

208

cedar beams line the ceiling end to end, and act as room dividers between the living room and kitchen. A huge stone fireplace catches my eye in the living room, the stone cascading all the way to the ceiling, covering the entire wall. My cabin is cozy...this cabin is grand.

I quickly remember my embarrassment and turn to Deputy May to apologize for the intrusion. I glance around and he is out of sight. Where did he go? It's hard to know in this place, it feels massive.

Mr. May speaks first, "Have a seat, Riley. Derek has spoken highly of you and we are glad to finally meet you...but I wasn't kidding around about just comin' to the front door. What exactly are you doing roaming around my barns at night?"

I cringe and stammer for a moment, feeling like a child being scolded, not a thirty-year-old woman who has put herself in the middle of an abduction, possibly murder, investigation. "I am so sorry Mr. May. I...I..."

Deputy May walks back into the room at that very moment, witnessing my sudden transformation into a child being punished. *Please God, drop a meteor on this house and end my embarrassment.* He interrupts my stammering and for that, I am grateful. "Dad, Riley is helping out the investigation of that missing woman out of Minwall. She used to be a police officer there before moving to Bearpoint."

"Oh! You didn't mention she's a cop too, Derek. I better watch what I say around these two, eh Jordan?" Jordan walks in to join the roast of Riley Morgen. Mr. May continues, "So what exactly does that have to do with my barns?"

Deputy May continues before I even have the chance to think up some soft version of the truth. "She has me on a suspect list and has to snoop around to check me off that list."

Mr. May burst out laughing, a deep belly laugh, had it not been at my expense I would have found it endearing. "Well, I told you to stop treading around lightly, acting all suspicious and just tell the girl you like her, Derek."

At this, both Deputy May and I burn scarlet red.

Mr. May saves us both the embarrassment of saying anything in response and continues talking. "Well Miss Riley. I am going to make you some hot chocolate. It's a little chilly out there tonight, and according to these two scoundrels, I make a hot chocolate worth sticking around for."

"That sounds lovely, Mr. May. Thank you so much."

I lock eyes with Deputy May and mouth 'I'm sorry'. It feels like a small, lame apology when I now have so much to apologize for. He mouths back 'me too' and even though I want to ask what he is apologizing for, I let it go and just smile. It feels good to be okay again. It's amazing how one friend can make you feel so much less alone.

Chapter Fifty-Three: Riley Morgen

I spent most of the night catching Deputy May up on everything that has happened in the last few weeks. He insists that I report the break in until I finally give in and explain that I think Sheriff Marks is involved somehow. He doesn't seem to agree, but at least he lets it go. He shows me the paperwork and internet searches that he and Jordan were focused on so intently when I was watching them through the window. They had continued looking into the cabins owned by LLCs in this area. It turns out most of them were pretty easy to research, vacation rentals that have ads a quick search online found. There are two that have not been so simple. Deputy May said he's working on them, and I didn't pry. I am just grateful for any help I can get.

Without realizing it, I managed to keep Deputy May up all night. The sun is just starting to peek out from the mountain range in the distance and I suddenly feel horrible for forcing someone else into my no sleep schedule.

"I can't believe we stayed up all night. Thanks again for welcoming a trespasser in, and for helping me out with the research...even after I was such a jerk to you. I'm sorry Derek, I should have trusted you."

"Trust is hard for cops. I get it. I'll drive you home."

I try to decline but Deputy May insists, and I find it easier to just give in. I think I might actually be tired, maybe this night with a friend did me some good...maybe I'll actually fall asleep for longer than a twenty-minute nap.

211

We get into Derek's truck, the first time I have seen him in something other than a patrol car, and drive down the long winding road toward my house. This is the road that sandwiches these properties with Binkin Trail. I stare out the passenger window, daydreaming in my worn-out state, looking forward to changing into some comfortable clothes and lying in my bed. The possibility of sleep is suddenly so enticing. Derek promptly slows the truck, causing me to snap out of my stupor and look out of the windshield. A runner is in the roadway, jogging toward us, moving to the far side of the road. Derek continues slowing and crosses into the opposite lane, giving the runner plenty of room. As we get closer to the figure, I glance over mindlessly and see the man, sweat pouring down his tanned skin, the droplets falling onto his black t-shirt...and his dark green joggers.

Dark green joggers.

"Stop the truck!" The desperation in my voice causing Deputy May's head to whip towards me.

"What is going on Riley?" He starts slowing down, his eyes never leaving the side of my face. He glances in the rearview mirror and continues, "There is a car comin' up behind me. What is going on Riley?"

"Just pull over. That runner. I need to talk to that runner."

With no further questions asked, Deputy May whips the truck around forcefully, turning around completely in one swift move and steps on the gas, speeding up toward the runner. He hits the button for his flashers and stops in the roadway, the runner not far ahead of us, seemingly unaware of the truck now stopped in the roadway behind him. I jump out of the vehicle and take off sprinting towards the runner, yelling "excuse me", with no response.

As I get closer, I notice the earbuds protruding from his ears...he must not hear me. I sprint in front of him and turn around quickly, causing him to stop abruptly.

His lips curl into an amused smile, "Well that's no fair, Riley Morgen. It's not a race if I don't even know you're there."

"Brady Bennett." I look him up and down, sure the disgust in my eyes is undisguised. I should have known the jogger was this creep.

"Have you come to join my run or do you and your deputy friend make it a habit to stop people who are minding their own business?"

"Were you minding your own business when you broke into my house yesterday?"

A light flickers in his eyes, a recognition of the truth. That eerie smirk appearing on his lips again. "I don't know what you're talking about. That sounds like something you should be talking to your deputy friend about, not your local hardware store clerk."

"I know it was you near Julia Preston's necklace on Binkin Trail. I know it was you following me in the woods that night. I know it was you in the woods near my house, watching me. I know it was you leaving threatening letters. I know it was you inside my house!" My voice starting as a scowl, rising with each sentence, I feel myself losing my composure.

Deputy May is walking towards us, his pace quickening, eyes locked on Brady in a predatory way. Brady turns, looking him up and down, clearly finding the scene quite amusing. He turns back to me before speaking again.

"No need to sic your deputy on me, Riley."

"Admit it to me. Admit it was you." I hiss.

213

"I've got to get going, I need to finish my run before work. It was good seeing you Riley Morgen…as always."

Brady begins to walk away. The anger is bubbling inside me, I know he is responsible for this.

I shout after him, "Where is Julia Preston?"

He stops and turns to face me. His face completely blank.

"I have no idea. Do you?"

He then turns and begins to run again.

Chapter Fifty-Four: Riley Morgen

If I thought I was exhausted before, I have learned a whole new meaning of the word since finding that letter in my bed. Even if I wanted to sleep, my body will not allow it knowing that someone was in my home, threatening to take my life. Each night, I lie in bed, clutching my firearm, waiting for a shadowy movement in the dark that has yet to come.

Julia swirls in my thoughts endlessly, and I do not believe she is dead... despite what dark green jogger's letter said. Criminals start to truly sweat when you get too close to the truth. I know this well enough to know...I must be getting close. Close to the truth. Close to Julia Preston. Close enough to be considered a threat to whoever it is leaving these letters...most likely, Brady Bennett. How is he connected to all of this? Why would he find me threatening enough to do all of this...unless he has Julia?

Sleep has become a foreign word, something I once knew so well, now something I can no longer grasp. Sometimes I think that may be for the better anyway. Somehow, I don't feel groggy or lost...I feel like everything is so clear. I have to push. I have to keep going until those last pieces suddenly snap into place. I have to find Julia Preston. Then I will let myself truly heal. I will go to therapy like my mother wants. I will start thinking about my future and stop putting so much of myself into the things that are in the past. I will do what I need to for myself. After I find Julia Preston.

My phone rings loudly, bringing me out of my deep thoughts and back into the present. Detective Ares' name appears on the screen, a photo of a younger Ares sitting at his first detective desk, flicking off the camera covering the screen. I quickly pick up the call and am met with his rushed voice.

"Ares, slow down. What are you talking about?"

"Sorry, I am in the middle of a million things." I hear a deep exhale before Ares starts talking again, "I was canvassing the area that Amanda Hutchings was last seen...talking to people, looking for cameras. One woman got an attitude with me, saying she doesn't know who Amanda is but that we need to be looking for her friend Krista. After some questioning, I got as much information as I could about a woman named Krista Redding who was last seen a few days ago."

"Ares...are you telling me there is another woman who vanished?"

"I am. Morgen...I found video of the last car to pick up Krista Redding. The license plate is clear as day and the car is seen leaving Minwall, getting on the highway, shortly after picking her up."

"That's incredible! So, you have a suspect of at least one possible abduction?"

"We do. After getting that plate, I ran it in Flock to see if the vehicle had been seen anywhere else in the city within the last few months, but there were no hits."

"Damn, so no luck tying it to any other cases yet."

"Nope. But here's the best part, Morgen."

Detective Ares pauses, the epitome of dramatic effect, while I silently wait.

He continues, "The vehicle comes back to a man in Bearpoint...and he lives near the area that Julia Preston's necklace was found."

I can barely speak as Detective Ares gives me all the details. The search warrant has already been granted, and will be executed early tomorrow morning.

My heart races, everything I have known all along is falling into place. The pieces are coming together. Julia Preston is here...and we are going to save her.

Chapter Fifty-Five: Julia Preston

The slam of the front door makes me sit straight up in bed. I can hear clanging in the kitchen. If I was not a prisoner locked in a bedroom, held hostage by a complete maniac, I would think we were being robbed right now. I tiptoe towards our bedroom door and press my ear against it, the memory of overhearing his last kill flooding my mind and sending a shiver through my body. Footsteps approaching the bedroom door. I jump backwards and wait to hear the metallic pinging of the padlock. After a few moments with no further sound, I chance it and put my ear to the door again.

I hear distant rustling noises, doors opening and closing. There is one more bedroom in this house. I have never been in it, and neither has Elaine. The old man never sleeps here as far as I have heard. Is it possible this is his bedroom? Are there more girls in that room? What is he doing in there? Heavy, uneven footsteps and grunts pass the wooden door pressed against the side of my face. The front door opens and closes. I hear a distant door close…more of a metal noise. A car door. The front door opens again and I hear loud banging across the floor. What is the old man doing? Elaine sits up in bed and raises her eyebrow at me.

"What is he doing?"

"I have no idea…I have a really sick feeling right now, Elaine. Something is really wrong."

Elaine actually laughs. "Everything is really wrong here…all the time."

218

The sound of sliding metal across the floor. I hear the old man grunting, his breaths heavy and labored. The jangling of his key ring. Is he about to open our door? No, it can't be…the sound is too far away. He must be opening the basement padlock. I swallow down the lump forming in my throat. He is probably getting another girl to torture and kill in some heinous way. Probably brought in new equipment for some abominable torture device, a new way of killing, to keep his interest. I have to hold on to the small hope that he will let Elaine and I go out to Minwall soon. I have to get these women out of here…I have to save us all.

I sit back on the bed, deciding I don't want to hear anything else, just in case another girl is coming upstairs to take her last terrified breaths. My heart doesn't want to know that there is someone else I couldn't save. I drape the blanket around my shoulders and curl up into a ball, lying on my bed, facing the wall. I don't want to hear what is happening out there. Even without the noise, my imagination refuses to just shut up.

Minutes or hours have passed; I have no idea. I remain a tiny ball of guilt and fear, wrapped in a cheap grey blanket. A key in the padlock of our door, the door swinging open suddenly. Elaine and I sit up quickly, blankets clutched to ourselves, eyes wide. The old man stands in the doorway, a wild and desperate look in his eyes.

"Get up now."

Chapter Fifty-Six: Riley Morgen

It is the night before Detective Ares is going to execute a search warrant that might result in Julia Preston going home, alive. I can't sleep. Sleep has been a rarity lately anyway, but at least tonight it's because of excitement instead of worry and paranoia. I knew he had something to do with this...I just hope Ares finds Julia alive. The letter can't be true. It will all be over soon. I don't even bother lying in bed feigning sleep tonight, I sit on the couch fully dressed, watching the eleven o'clock news. Detective Ares invited me to come by to witness the search warrant, and I plan on being there bright and early...at the very least to look in his eyes while it all comes crumbling down around him.

The night seems to be dragging; we are so close to finding her. I know it. A loud knock at the front door causes me to nearly jump out of my skin, my head whipping around and staring at the wood. Who is here in the middle of the night? At least I know it isn't the burglar, suddenly finding his manners and coming to the front door like a normal person. I peek out the window and see Deputy May standing on my porch, looking antsy, head turning constantly, looking for some unseen entity in the night.

"Derek, what are you doing here?"

He pushes past me and propels the front door closed, making sure it is locked. He looks frantic.

"Riley, I think I fucked up."

"What are you talking about?"

"Remember that I told you there were still two LLCs that I was looking into?"

"Of course."

"I did everything I could to find any information, but it just had me going in circles. There was no registered agent listed, no public information that I could access at all. I put in a formal request with the secretary of state's office weeks ago for owner information."

I stare at Derek intensely; I have never seen him look flustered. Whatever he is about to tell me has him near panicked.

He continues, "I got the request back today. One of them is just some long winded trail leading to a vacation rental like the rest."

"And the other?" My heart is pounding, filling my ears with the noise of a drum.

"Deer Keep LLC...it's owned by Gerald Marks."

"Sheriff Marks?"

"Yes."

"Is that where he lives?"

"No Riley, no. I have been to his house, and it's not that cabin. Why would he have some random cabin that he needs to hide under an LLC?" He sounds distraught.

"There could be a bunch of reasons, I guess. Legal protection for a rental cabin, not wanting anyone to know it is owned by the Sheriff so he doesn't end up getting sued by some money hungry renters. Or he could be keeping women prisoner there. It's a wide spectrum."

Deputy May does not seem to appreciate my joke. He looks more worried by the minute.

"May, do you want to go over there and peep in the windows? We both know how good I am at trespassing on people's property unnoticed."

"Riley, I confronted him."

"What?" Now I am the one being flooded with panic.

"I confronted him and we got into an argument over it. He fired me."

"He fired you for asking about a cabin he owns?"

"He fired me because he said I am meddling in an investigation that our department has nothing to do with. He gave me an order to stay out of it when you found the locket...I didn't listen."

I run to my bedroom and grab the black hooded sweatshirt off my bed, throwing it over my head while rushing towards Deputy May.

"What are you doing Riley?"

"Derek, we have to go to that cabin. This is not about you meddling in Minwall Police Department's investigation. This is about you meddling in something the sheriff doesn't want anyone to know. We need to find out what that is, right now."

Chapter Fifty-Seven: Riley Morgen

Deputy May has the gas pedal pressed to the floor, his truck tires squealing with each bend in the road.

"Faster, Derek."

"I'm going as fast as I can, Riley. I'm not tryin' to kill us both on the way there."

"You have him panicked. The most dangerous criminal is a panicked one."

Derek turns the truck hard into a dirt driveway, dust flying, the view in front of us lined with tall grass and fallen trees. The cabin begins to come into view. It is small and run down, the windows covered with wooden boards.

"Is this just an abandoned property?" Derek asks.

"He wouldn't have gotten so defensive if it was. There's a truck around back, is that his?"

"Yeah, that's definitely his. He's here."

Derek stops the truck, blocking the dirt driveway and we both get out, silently taking in the property. The sheriff's truck is empty, so he must be inside. I glance at the cabin again and get chills. There is nothing innocent that is done in a place like this. It looks like something straight out of a horror film. I mean honestly, who would even want to be in this building?

We creep around the building, realizing every window is boarded up and there is only one door.

"Do you think we should just watch or go knock on the door?" As soon as the question leaves Deputy May's lips, I hear the front door of the cabin opening. I shove him against the side of the house, listening. I know we will not have long before Sheriff Marks sees Deputy May's truck, but the element of surprise is always a plus.

I hear a woman's voice first. "I can't walk around with her cuffed, do you realize how that looks? You need to take them off."

Sheriff Marks responds, "You need to shut your fucking mouth, girl, before I decide you will never speak again. Stick to the fucking plan. I won't say it again."

Deputy May's eyes go wide and I press a finger to my lips, reminding him, not a word. The more we hear right now, the better. Instantaneously, he taps the side of his nose with his finger, and furrows his brow. I breathe deep and realize what he is trying to alert me to…the smell of smoke in the air.

I glance around, looking for billows of gray smoke or orange dancing flames to alert me to where exactly the smell is coming from, back still pressed against the cabin wall. Two women unexpectantly come running into view, sprinting for the woods. The first is small and frail, a black hoodie pulled up around her head. I know that hoodie too well. *It is Elaine.* What exactly is Sheriff Marks doing with Elaine? Close behind her runs another woman, hands bound in front of her, metal handcuffs catching a glint in the moonlight. Her once golden-brown hair is limp, dull and dirty, body ravaged and weak. I can only hope that the clothing she wears is oversized, that her malnourished body has not become that small.

That is Julia Preston.

Everything I have given myself to over the last few months suddenly comes to a head. All of the lost sleep, the threats, the nightmares, everything I have been through because of my career as a police officer. Everything I now am because of my career as a police officer. I have given so much of myself because of these exact moments. The moment when despite all odds, despite the police department losing hope, despite the media moving on to a newer, more sensationalized story, a victim is found alive.

I forget myself, forget my own safety when I sprint into the darkness and scream, "Elaine!"

Elaine stops abruptly just feet from the wood line. She turns and we lock eyes. This is the moment where I will know the truth. Is Elaine a victim of the sheriff? Or is she, his accomplice?

"Officer Morgen?"

"Elaine, I've told you, just call me Riley."

Elaine grabs Julia's wrist, the metal of the handcuff chain clanking. She guides Julia, stepping slowly towards me, seemingly so unsure of who to trust, questioning if I am some starvation induced hallucination. Julia looks terrified...and so, so tiny. I feel a pang in my chest as she steps into the moonlight, and I see the extent of this man's damage. Gone is the girl in the flowing green sundress. The girl whose smile conveyed an easy and beautiful life. He has stolen that from her. I find myself wondering what else this man has stolen from her...the things that cannot be seen.

I have to ask the question that I already know the answer to. The question that I have been longing to ask for these seemingly endless months. "Are you Julia Preston?"

Her hazel eyes dart between Elaine and I, as if needing confirmation that I am someone who can be trusted. Elaine nods her head almost imperceptibly. Julia speaks in a meek, tender voice, "Yes, I am."

I am thrown back into the reality around me as I hear a shout and a gun shot. I whirl around; eyes scanning for Deputy May and find him and the sheriff wrestling on the ground. I sprint towards him, only to be met with his shout, "I got this Riley! Check the house!"

I turn to make sure that Elaine and Julia haven't disappeared and find them standing only a few feet behind me. They must have followed me to help Deputy May. Somehow that feels so reassuring. We are in this together now. I head for the front door, thick smoke now billowing out from the cabin.

I hear Julia's voice behind me, still tender, but seemingly has found some hidden strength. "There are other girls in there! We have to help!" She takes off running for the house, I call for her, trying to stop her from going into a literal burning building.

I lift my hoodie and rip my undershirt in strips, handing one to Elaine and wrap a strip around my nose and mouth. "Where does he keep the other girls?"

"In the basement."

I sprint into the smoke-filled cabin, dropping to my knees and crawling low on the ground, hoping to avoid the smoke racing for the open front door. Elaine runs to the left and I pause, considering if I should follow her since I have no idea where I am going. I see the outline of her figure returning through the smoke, a large set of keys swinging from her hand. I follow close behind her, grabbing her shoulder so she knows she is not alone. Julia's emaciated figure comes into view, banging and throwing herself into a large wooden door,

226

padlock swinging tauntingly with each hit. Elaine shoves her aside and starts fitting various keys into the lock, swearing softly every time it doesn't turn. What could only be a minute feels like an hour. We don't have much time, the cabin is filling with smoke, even though I see no flames yet.

The basement door bursts open, swinging wildly, with a loud thud against the wall, it stops. Smoke pouring from the dark chasm, I clutch the piece of shirt against my mouth harder, and focus on shallow breaths. This is just like being exposed to CS gas in my police training, focus on shallow breaths. My eyes sting and burn with the smoke, I squint, letting them water heavily. We don't have much time. I don't know what I will see down there, but we only have minutes left before at least one of us loses consciousness.

I pull the small flashlight from my jeans pocket and run down the stairs into the darkness. Flicking on my light, I quickly scan around. The air is filled with soot and particles of dirt, the darkness seeming to swallow the light of my flashlight. An unfinished basement, dirt floor and walls surrounding me. This looks like a literal hole hand dug underneath the house...possibly a cellar from a hundred years ago. A barrel in the center of the room, smoke swirling from the fire inside it. It smells chemical. We need to hurry. Women in dog cages. A line of cages from wall to wall. Women folded up in dog cages, hardly big enough for a German Sheppard, let alone a human being. *You don't have time.* I quickly snap out of my shock and see Elaine already forcing keys into cages, trying her hardest to get them open quickly. She clutches her mouth and nose with one hand, clearly the smoke is getting to her. Julia grabs the set of keys from her hand and continues her work, pushing Elaine low to the ground where she puts her face into the dirt, taking small, shallow breaths. Julia's hands still cuffed together, the metal of her cuffs twisting and clacking against the metal bars of the cage.

The first lock opens and I rip at the top of the cage so aggressively, I feel a rusty bar slice open my palm. I throw the top somewhere in the darkness and grab the woman inside. Her eyes are barely open, her skin so warm, breathing labored. I muster every bit of strength I have and lift her from the cage. I am surprised at the absence of weight in my arms as I lower her to the dirt floor. I loop my arms underneath her armpits and link my fingers together. I begin dragging her toward the stairs, her limp head bobbing freely. Julia continues making work of the cages while Elaine jumps to her feet, rushing to help me. She grabs the woman's ankles and we go as quickly as we can up the stairs. We spill her onto the grass just outside the front door and run back for the basement. I can still hear Deputy May and Sheriff Marks yelling, fighting.

As my feet hit the first steps of the basement, I hear another gun shot. *Please let Derek be okay. Please let Derek be okay.* That's the thing about being a police officer. You know that you could lose your life doing this job at any moment. And you still do it. You know that your partner could lose their life at any moment, which is somehow so much scarier than the idea of losing your own, but you have to trust that they will rely on their training...that they will be okay. If I worry about Deputy May right now, my focus won't be on what is front of me. I trust that he will be okay, and he trusts that I will too. It's all you can do.

I jump the last few steps, my knees nearly buckling as my feet slam into the dirt. Julia now has two more cages open. She is working on one more, the final two cages sit empty in the left side of the room. Were those cages once filled by Julia and Elaine? I glance between the two open cages. One woman is lifting herself, clearly in terrible pain, but determined. The other woman lies against the dirt and metal bars underneath her. She is not moving. Is she dead? I have no idea, and not enough time to worry about checking right now. I help the first woman pull herself to her full height, then grab the other woman and lift her from her prison. Alive or dead, she will not be left in this hell-on-earth. I begin dragging her, Elaine helping the first woman close behind us. I drop the limp woman in the grass and quickly check her pulse. It is faint. I press my finger beneath her nose and feel her shallow breaths against my flesh.

There is one more girl, and Julia. I take a few deep breaths of unsoiled, outside air and race back inside, my eyes singed from the smoke. When I make it to the basement, Julia is frantically pulling the last lock.

"It won't open! Help!" She coughs and gags.

The woman inside the cage is terrified. She is screaming for help, eyes locked on mine, begging me for life.

I grab the cage and start to pull it towards the stairs. "Help!" I scream, to Julia, to Elaine, to anyone that can hear us. I cough against the torn shirt around my face. My lungs are begging for air. Elaine and Julia grab the opposite end of the cage and we begin dragging it up the stairs. As we reach the top, a wave of dizziness forces itself upon me and my legs buckle.

229

The three of us, pulling the final cage to safety, our blackened smoke-filled lungs and the faint sound of sirens in the distance.

Those are the last things I remember.

Chapter Fifty-Eight: Him

I wake to yelling outside of my house. It isn't the kind of yelling that I prefer, the soul soothing screams of a life coming to its inevitable end...perhaps earlier than expected. No, it is the kind that I believed I would never hear.

"Minwall Police Department! Search Warrant! Open the door or we will force entry!"

I hear my brother and father stirring from sleep. This is my brother's doing, I know it. His meddling has led to this somehow and he will pay for this. He forgets that I am always in control. The yelling begins again.

"Minwall Police Department! Search Warrant! Open the door or we will force entry!"

I rise from bed, not in the mood to have to fix a broken front door later, planning to open it and figure out my way out of all this. I hear my brother has beaten me to it.

"What is all this? What is going on?" My brother inquires.

"Show me your hands and step out onto the porch." A gruff order.

The sounds of clicking handcuffs.

My brother speaks again, "What is going on? Am I under arrest?"

"We have a search warrant for your property; you are being detained while we execute the search. You will receive an executed copy of the paperwork upon the completion of our search, detailing the items seized." I hear the rustling of papers before the police officer's voice again, "Is there anyone else in the residence?"

"Yes, my brother and our father."

Ah, my cue. I'm not in the mood to be manhandled today, so I slowly open my bedroom door and begin the walk down the hallway. I raise my hands above my head and announce myself to avoid any bullshit. I know how trigger happy some cops can be.

After police have placed my father and I in cuffs, they lead each of us into the front yard and we are seated on the ground. My brother is still asking questions...he just doesn't learn. I have one question for him, "Can you shut your fucking mouth for once in your damned existence?" but I refrain from saying anything. Silence is always best in the presence of police. My father has not said a word. I am truly my father's son.

I watch, silently seated in the grass, handcuffed, wearing nothing but a pair of sweatpants, as a team of police officers enter my home. The home that has been in my family for generations. The home that helped to create who my father is, in turn helping to create who I am. The home that has seen the last moments of more women than I could count. I have never asked my father if he knows his kill number...I didn't want that type of competitive nature between us. I have heard so many stories, since I was a child, never hearing the same story twice...he must have a respectable number, like me. I briefly wonder if my father would be dumb enough to keep any mementos or evidence, then silently scold myself for thinking I know better than the master of this craft.

He has taught me everything I know...there will be no evidence in either of our bedrooms. Are they looking for the

232

same girl Riley Morgen is? She has never set foot on my property; there will be no link connecting her to me. No...I don't think that has anything to do with this. No. I think this is exactly what has to happen because of my prying brother. I could answer that question just by requesting the search warrant paperwork, but I refuse to say anything. Cops only know what you tell them. Whether by speaking to them, or leaving evidence behind. I refuse to even show a facial expression that may give someone an idea about me. The only slip up I have ever made, was completely intentional. I will be walking away from this, no matter what.

A search warrant is not a quick process. I sit on my front lawn until I lose the feeling in my fingers, bent against the grass, trapped behind my back by a pair of metal restraints. The handcuffs were not locked, and have become too tight as I have moved around. Either an amateur move by this cop, or done purposely to let me accidently inflict my own pain. Make me talk, request to loosen the cuffs. I don't mind the pain honestly. It gives me something else to think about for the hours I sit here waiting. It makes it easier to avoid feeding into the anger I want to unleash on my brother at this moment.

My brother looks so nervous, still. He makes all of this so easy. The cops each glance at him every so often, clearly thinking he looks guilty. I'm embarrassed to be related to this sorry excuse of a man. How dare he wear *my* face. I am immediately taken back to a time when we were ten years old. At that time, we were still brothers, our differences had not created two completely different, identical people quite yet. We used to run through the woods, laughing and throwing sticks, hiding from each other and jumping out to make the other scream. We were regular boys...rowdy boys if you listened to our mother. When I found her body, still tucked into her bed one morning, I never felt panic. My brother was too panicked to function. He scrunched himself into a ball in the corner of our living room, watching as the police and EMTs trekked through our house, dirty boot marks in the carpet and lingering questions floating in the air. I never felt a thing other than anger...at my mother for leaving us. At my brother for being so useless...for leaving me to deal with everything while he cowered in a corner, melting away from reality and pretending that it just wasn't real. Here he is, twenty years later, scrunched into that tiny nothingness in the grass, dirty boots trekking through our living room again. He might as well still be ten years old...nothing about him has changed.

Officers come and go, in and out of the house, occasionally carrying brown paper bags and boxes filled with whatever they have decided proves what they think they know. Go ahead and built your case, officers. I'll wait right here.

I suddenly realize that the search of the house itself has started to slow down, the team of investigators thinning. Where have they all gone? I casually glance about the property, my eyes stopping on a group of officers standing in front of the second barn. So, they did their research of the property...the barns are in play. Well, there is no doubt that the barn will offer a life sentence's worth of evidence. *You're welcome, detective.*

Remain in control of yourself. Control the narrative at all times. They are playing into your hand.

A familiar looking detective approaches my brother, nodding to the officer babysitting him. The officer lifts my brother to his feet and the detective introduces himself.

"I am Detective Ares from the Minwall Police Department and I am investigating the murder and disappearance of numerous women that I believe are all connected."

My brother looks like he is going to be sick. His eyes dart around, looking for somewhere to land that will feel less threatening, no doubt. He clears his throat and speaks, "Okay."

Real prolific, brother. They're going to quote that for the 20/20 special, no doubt.

Detective Ares continues, "Your vehicle was seen picking up Krista Redding, who went missing out of Minwall."

"That's impossible."

Detective Ares continues as if my brother had said nothing at all. It is clear this is not an interrogation; this is someone providing irreputable information. "During the execution of our search warrant, evidence was found on your property that proves your involvement in Krista Redding's abduction."

"Wait! What? You have this all wrong. Let me explain."

"Brady Bennett, you are under arrest for the abduction of Krista Redding. Based on evidence found during our search, you can expect a murder charge to be added as well in due time."

Brady begins to pull at the officer holding his arm, "Wait, it wasn't me!"

Detective Ares nods to the officer holding Brady's arm, and he is led to a nearby police car and placed in the back. Brady continues yelling, protesting his innocence as the door to the patrol car closes in his face.

Detective Ares walks toward me and my father, both of us being forced to our feet by our babysitting officers. I can feel the blood rushing back to my fingers, my wrists throbbing.

"Gentlemen, my name is Detective Ares with the Minwall Police Department. I apologize for the intrusion on your home. I have some questions about your whereabouts last Thursday night."

My father speaks immediately, "No problem, Detective, we are happy to help however we can. Jack and I went hunting near the mountains on Thursday. Ended up camping for the night. I still have all the gear in my truck actually. Can I ask you what exactly Brady was involved in?"

Thankfully, I am a man that is always in control. My facial expression does not differ in even the smallest ways. I am so proud of my dad...of course he would be ready with an alibi at any possible moment.

"We believe he is involved with the abduction of a woman in Minwall."

"I knew it. I knew there was something really wrong with that boy...I didn't want to believe he would actually hurt someone...but there is something not right with him, sir. There's been times that I have been genuinely scared of him." My father's eyes drop to the floor, a look of disappointment and hurt flashes across his face. *The master has still got it.*

Detective Ares nodded and continued, "I need both of you to come down to the precinct and answer a few questions, formally."

My father glances at me, then feigns worry, "I don't know anything about this, Detective...Brady is sick. I'm ashamed to admit that I often wished we had only had Jack. Once their mom died, I just couldn't handle him on my own anymore...I couldn't control him. I'm so sorry." My father hangs his head in shame, clearly near tears, as his voice shakes so convincingly. This man deserves an Oscar.

"You don't have anything to apologize for Mr. Bennett. Brady is a grown man and is in control of his own actions. Based on video, witnesses and evidence found here today, we know that Brady is our offender. The two of you have nothing to worry about, I just need to ask a few questions on the record about your whereabouts and if you know any details about his whereabouts during specific times."

"I understand, Detective. We are happy to help however we can, right Jack?"

I nod and respond, "Of course, sir."

Chapter Fifty-Nine: Riley Morgen

I wake in an all-white room, the sunlight beaming into my face from a large window nearly covering the entire wall. I am momentarily blinded and my eyes sting and water with the sparkling intrusion. My other senses begin to wake from my deep slumber and I hear a steady beep. The smell of smoke stains the insides of my nostrils. *Smoke. The cabin.* I force my eyes open against the light and glance around the room. I am in a hospital room, ballons and flowers scattered about the lone table directly across from me. I look around my bed and find the remote, clicking the button to call for a nurse.

A few seemingly eternal minutes later, a young blond woman wearing a leopard print scrub top walks into my room.

"Good morning, Miss Riley, we're glad to see you up." She greets me with a chipper smile.

Miss Riley. A pang in my chest. "Where is Deputy May? Is he okay?"

She smiles sweetly at me, a hand on her hip and says, "Yes ma'am, he is just fine. He's been asking about you too. I'll let him know you're up."

The sweet nurse checks my vitals and informs me that everyone from the cabin ended up coming here to this hospital. I was treated for smoke inhalation and expected to make a full recovery within a few days. She also mentioned a tetanus shot for a nasty cut on my hand, and I refrained from telling her it came from the rusty cages that held those women

238

prisoner. Apparently, I slept for an entire day afterwards, though I suspect that had nothing to do with the smoke inhalation and everything to do with not sleeping for the last week or so. I still feel groggy. I am not convinced my brain has actually woken up yet.

After the nurse leaves my room, I hear a small knock on my door and Deputy May enters.

"I'm glad you're okay, Riley."

"I'm glad you're okay, Derek."

He stood beside my bed, holding my unbandaged hand. The two of us said nothing for a long while, just staring into the other's eyes, silently conveying a story too heavy to repeat right now.

****

I was released from the hospital after three days and felt good as new. Mostly because the boredom allowed me to get a lot of much needed sleep. Each of the girls that were kept in those cages fared much worse than I did. Julia was treated for severe malnutrition and dehydration, as were all the girls except Elaine. Elaine seemed to be given more food than any of the other girls...I wasn't sure I wanted to know the reason why. The women that were left in the cages suffered severe smoke inhalation, and came very close to dying that day. Each was covered in bruises and wounds given to them by the monster who held them captive. They would later give full statements detailing the physical and sexual abuse they each endured.

After I lost consciousness in the cabin, Elaine and Julia dragged me to safety. They saved my life, and they each remind me that I saved theirs that day too.

Deputy May managed to get Sheriff Marks into custody, and suffered only a graze wound to his right arm from the first of the gun shots I heard during the whole ordeal. Gerald Marks attempted to shoot him a number of times as they wrestled. Luckily, Deputy May overpowered Marks and held his wrist to the ground while they fought for control. Nothing that a Band-Aid couldn't fix, Deputy May reminded me.

Sheriff Marks' property has now become a massive crime scene, with bodies dating back to before I was even born. Apparently, he has been killing women in that cabin at least as long as he has been in law enforcement, likely even longer. The cabin once belonged to his father, and Ares believes it is where Marks lived as a child. He hid ownership under an LLC many years ago, probably when it became more of a graveyard than a home. The tally of bodies found around the property grows every day, and it will probably be a while before we know the true extent of his carnage. He will never be outside of prison walls again, that we know for sure.

His truck was packed with all sorts of supplies and evidence. According to Elaine, he knew that the police were getting too close to him and had decided to leave town and start a new life somewhere else. A lot of the supplies in the truck indicated that he may have planned on living in the remote wilderness somewhere, probably figuring they could lay low long enough for any manhunt to die down. He planned to allow all the women in the basement to die from smoke inhalation, but apparently didn't have the heart to let the cabin actually burn down. It was a controlled fire that was meant to fill the basement with smoke long enough to kill the caged women...then smolder out on its own eventually. Somehow that run down pile of wood and memories meant so much more than actual human lives. I assume that means he thought he would be going back eventually. Elaine explained the reason that he chose to keep her and Julia alive...he planned to use them as bait to bring home new victims, so he wouldn't have to pay Brady Bennett to abduct women anymore.

Julia was reunited with her family at the hospital, and her mother came to visit me soon after I woke up. I always hated my experiences with a victim's family, so heavy with fear, blame and desperation. Mrs. Preston gave me the best experience I have ever had in that hospital room...an experience to start the healing of all the others. She held my hand and cried for a long time. She repeated that she didn't know how to thank me for never giving up on Julia. She felt so motherly to me, and for once I didn't hate the emotions filling the room. For once, I let myself cry too.

Elaine did not have anyone visit her in the hospital, except Julia's mother. Detective Ares told me that Elaine will be moving in with Julia and going back to school. She never wants to live on the streets again, and Julia said she will never let her. It touched me seeing their bond. Sometimes all it takes is one bond like that to get you through the worse trauma you could ever imagine.

Detective Ares filled me in on all the details of the search warrant on Brady Bennett's house. The most disturbing being a woman's preserved skin being found. Not some pieces of skin. Her entire, intact, skin. A skin suit. Apparently, the officers that found it took some time off and were sent to the department psychiatrist. I don't even want to know about the nightmares that come with that one.

There were firearms and knives seized and sent to the lab for testing. That will take months before we hear any results. One of the barns had dried blood all over the floor and one wall, which is being tested against Krista Redding's DNA. Her decapitated head and body were found charred in the firepit behind the barns. Some distinctive dental work allowed Minwall Police Department to identify her prior to any DNA testing. Just like Sheriff Gerald Marks' property, the Bennett property is still being searched, looking for bodies. The number of bodies has not yet been finalized, but at this point Brady is facing two murder charges, two counts of human trafficking and four counts of abduction...he has denied involvement in all of it and maintains his innocence. According to Detective Ares, the investigation is just getting started, and they are looking at many past cases for possible links to Brady Bennett.

Julia Preston and Elaine Montalto both identified Brady Bennett as the man who abducted them from Minwall and sold them to Gerald Marks. The scar on his face stood out to each of them during their abductions, and Julia stated that the scar was 'burned in her mind', it was something she would never forget. The other survivors identified Elaine as bringing them to the cabin, she had told them there was a John willing to pay large amounts of money and drugs for a few days long date. When Elaine was questioned by Detective Ares about being involved in the human trafficking of these women, Elaine explained everything. She was kept alive because she agreed to do this, her life was threatened constantly if she made even a small mistake or tried to get any help. Elaine had planned to use this as a chance to escape, but decided she could not leave Julia Preston behind, because of the bond that formed between the two of them. She convinced Gerald Marks that Julia could help Elaine with new girls. This is the reason Julia Preston was kept alive.

The District Attorney was informed of Elaine's assistance in this case, and the state refused to prosecute. In the eyes of the state, Elaine is a victim who was forced into criminal activity in order to maintain her survival. Some of the victim's families disagree with this decision and blame Elaine specifically for the deaths of their daughters. I wouldn't be surprised if she will be facing civil lawsuits in the future.

No one could explain how Julia Preston's locket ended up on Binkin Trail. Elaine stated that she had never seen a necklace on Julia, the three months or more of their friendship was in complete darkness. She did not even know what Julia looked like for the majority of their captivity. Julia stated that she was wearing it when she left for her run, the day she was abducted. She remembers being in the vehicle with Brady Bennett, then waking up in the dog cage. She had never seen Binkin Trail the entire time she was kept in Bearpoint. During Brady's questioning, Detective Ares asked about Julia's locket. He denied having any knowledge of the necklace. Even though I never saw his face that day, I did see the outfit of the runner ahead of me on Binkin Trail the day I found the locket. The clothing was the same as the day I confronted Brady running on the street near his home. I believe it was Brady that day...but I can't explain why he would be dropping the necklace on Binkin Trail. It was the single thing that led to the downfall of Sheriff Gerald Marks and Brady Bennett.

Chapter Sixty: Julia Preston

After spending a week in the hospital, I was finally able to go back to my apartment in Minwall. My mother didn't want to let me out of her sight, and I didn't blame her. I insisted that Elaine move in with me so she could work on starting a new life, and after some convincing, she agreed. We became family in that darkness, and I wasn't going to abandon her now that we were in the light. I now know that it is thanks to Elaine that I am still alive. When we were in the cages, I was convinced that knowing she was there with me was keeping me going...and it did. But only now do I realize the true extent of everything, had she not convinced Gerald Marks to keep me alive, he probably wouldn't have. Especially for that long.

I lived in that cabin for four months. My mother never gave up hope, never stopped looking. The woman who rescued us, Riley Morgen, said that Elaine had been missing for nearly two years, but had never even been reported as missing. I cringe when I think about it. I don't want to imagine the things that Elaine had gone through while she was there, but my brain forces me to all the time. My mother insisted on paying for both Elaine and I to go to therapy. Elaine looked more terrified at that suggestion than I had ever seen her look in the cabin.

It's true that I will never be the same person that was abducted off the street while on an early morning run. I had an innocence then that I never even realized...until it was taken from me. I haven't gone for a run since coming home, I don't even want to leave the house alone. My therapist says it will take time for me to reacclimate to some normalcy again. I feel better that both the man that abducted us, and the man that kept us prisoner, are now in prison themselves. The trial won't be for some time still, but I know they will be there for a very, very long time. For that, I am thankful.

I will only admit this to my therapist, but I am not angry that this happened to me. I don't have any regrets about running alone that morning, and I refuse to see myself as some poor pathetic girl who was caged, starved and brainwashed. I am alive. I survived and I helped save every other girl that day. Through all of it, I was given Elaine. A friendship and love that I will never feel for anyone else. She saved me in so many ways, and I will do everything to help her find her dreams out here, in normal life. As crazy as it sounds, I think I was meant to be abducted that day. Meant to be caged and tortured. If I wasn't there, how would all of this have turned out? Would those girls have made it out alive...or would they be yet another body buried on that property? Would Gerald Marks and Brady Bennett still be free men, instead of locked away, where they belong? Would Elaine have made it out alive?

There are a lot of girls that no one saved. The police have been searching both properties for weeks, and are still excavating bodies. Gerald Marks was truly a monster.

And I...I am a survivor.

Chapter Sixty-One: Elaine

That Minwall detective asked me about Julia's necklace. I had to lie. I couldn't tell him I took it off of her...because then I'd have to explain how I had access to it before Julia ever woke up in that cage. I didn't help kidnap Julia. A girl like that never would have gotten in a car with a girl like me. That's why the old man had to pay big bucks for girls like Julia. I bet he didn't pay nothin' close to that for me...I was probably so high, I would have gone to his house for nothin' more than the promise of one more hit.

I helped the old man put Julia in her cage after she first arrived. He was so excited when he saw her, like he couldn't wait to take the light from her eyes. He was basically wiping the drool from his lips. It made me sick. I knew that look too well...the look of a predator. When he wasn't looking, I took the necklace off her and slipped it in my pocket. I knew a girl like that would have family looking for her. People who actually give a shit about her. Maybe I was a little jealous. But I knew I could use that. I knew if I dropped the necklace, it would make them look here. It would be easy enough to do one night when I brought a new girl home.

I never cared about being rescued, I knew I could promise to bring home another girl one day and then never come back. I knew I would leave on my own eventually, when I was ready. I gotta be really honest here, and it's gunna make me sound pretty fucked up. But I never cared about saving any of those girls. I never once felt bad about bringing girls to their

246

deaths. They shouldn't have been so stupid to think driving out to some cabin in the woods to meet a John was anything other than a death trap, an obvious set up. They deserved it at that point honestly. No marks on my conscience.

The girls were just causalities in a bigger game. The old man needed to go down. That piece of shit grew to represent everything I ever hated in my life. He was my father, beating my mother senseless, leaving her lying on the floor crying out my name. He was my mother, too high to recognize her own daughter, selling me to men for drugs or rent money. He was every single man that held down my twelve-year-old self and took what he wanted, took the only bit of innocence left from me. At first, I thought I could take him down, make him pay, have him sitting in a prison for the rest of his life. Just like my father. As time went on, as I saw everything that Gerald Marks really is, I knew it was not enough. I wanted him dead. I needed to be the one to do it.

I should have left long before Julia was caged. But I couldn't. I began planning how I would kill him...how satisfying the drip of his blood down my fingers would be. I was here to rip his beating heart from his chest and bite into it, consuming the very core of him. I couldn't leave before my destiny was fulfilled. I needed this. For every single time people in my life had failed me.

Then Julia came. She became this light in the darkness that had surrounded me since my earliest memories. I had never felt this way before. It was another being who cared about me...not what I could give her, or what she could take from me...she just cared that I was alive and happy. When I realized it, it was the most overwhelming thing I had ever

247

experienced. I realized I had been dead inside. I don't think I was ever alive. Until Julia.

She softened my edges and woke up parts of me that I didn't believe existed...specifically, my heart. She became a friend. A sister. A human being that deserved protection and love and a life outside of that cage.

I still wanted Gerald Marks dead, but I knew I had to get Julia to safety first.

In all of this, my only regret is that he is still breathing.

Chapter Sixty-Two: Sheriff Gerald Marks

The killing started a long, long time ago when I was in my early twenties. I married very young, high school sweethearts who dreamed of nothin' more than a house full of kids and a long life of lovin' each other. She was the first person in my life to truly love me...and the last. I often look back on my life and wonder if things would have been different, had I not lost her. I wasn't always like this. I wasn't always a monster, a beast, a shell of a human being. Rebecca was the love of my life, and when she was diagnosed with cancer at the age of twenty, a piece of me snapped. Slowly, as her body died, so did I.

When I buried her, I knew that fundamentally, I was different. I couldn't put my finger on it at the time, but I knew that something in me had shattered. Shattered in a way that can't be super glued back together again. Like when mama's favorite vase breaks and you do your very best to glue it back together, but there's those small slivers missin'. You know it will never be the same, but you do your best to pretend it's just as good and you hide all the cracks by turning the vase so the bad side doesn't show. The vase now wears a mask for the world to see, everything is fine...nothing has changed, and then one day something comes along and strains all those little cracks until the whole thing shatters again. Then you think...it's not even worth the glue to try to put it back together. *It's just too broken.*

I was so angry at the world for taking Rebecca from me. I spent years letting myself fill with hate until I felt nothing else. The only release I ever felt was when I have a life in my hands. It stopped mattering who it was or if they had ever wronged me personally, they were just where God put them and I was me, a predator waiting for prey.

The decision to run for sheriff wasn't really my own. It actually came from John Bennett. You see, him and I, we were alike in our extracurricular activities. I was perfectly happy being nothin' more than a cop, hunting prey in my off time, layin' low best I could. John knew we needed more safety than that. We needed power in this town. So, I ran, never expecting to win, and did the job for twenty seven of the thirty-five years I've been wearin' this uniform.

As age got the better of us both, John approached me with a business proposition that I could not refuse. His son, Jack, was like us. He was fifteen at the time, and John had been showing him the ropes. Helping him with his first few kills. John decided that Jack would make this his business, he would bring me girls and I pay a discounted fee, in order to look the other way on his nefarious activities. You see, Jack never quite knew the extent of just how blood soaked my past really is. He just knew I was like his daddy...like him. I think that was enough for a young boy. I would have looked the other way without the discount of course, but I think John was trying to be a good father, teach him the way the world is. I think John was just trying to teach the boy some responsibility, give him a positive outlet for the urges he was born with. Teach him some form of control and help him set up a future.

The last fifteen years have been a very healthy business relationship between Jack and I. But here's the hard truth. I'm gettin' to be an old man now. I'm still all there upstairs but my body just can't fight the way it used to. Powerful still, sure, but not quite swift on my feet anymore. I want to retire and live out my days in that cabin, doing the only thing that brought me feeling since I lost Rebecca. Problem is, girls ain't cheap. Then one day I came up with the most brilliant plan. Why couldn't the girls work for me? Women inherently trust other women. I don't have to pay anything, and can have constantly full cages. It was all working so well, until that damn girl came to Bearpoint. Women always think they can stick their nose wherever they want it. Always think they can make things better, make things right. That damn girl, Riley Morgen, ruined everything. Over forty years of work in that cabin and now they're digging up my property, tearing it apart piece by piece, like it didn't take the blood of my father and my grandfather to build. Like the blood of all those women is worth more than that.

She thinks she's so damn smart, but I will have the last laugh. I may be in prison, but the next generation of killer will continue his reign. Meanwhile his innocent brother will serve out the sentence. Something tells me this is exactly how John Bennett always wanted it.

Chapter Sixty-Three: Brady Bennett

I am innocent. I am really getting tired of saying it...I just wish someone would believe me. There is video of my car picking up that girl that was found in the firepit behind our barns. They said she was decapitated. I can't believe anyone thinks I would do this. The detective has pictures of me in the car with her that night, driving to Bearpoint from Minwall. Only it wasn't me...it was my brother. I tried to tell them it wasn't me, but no one believes me. Then two of the girls identified me in a line up. I am screwed. I am going to spend the rest of my life in prison, for something I didn't do. Something my brother did.

I admitted to the detective that I was in the woods that night, following Riley Morgen. I admitted that it was me leaving her those threatening letters. So, I'm guilty of breaking and entering. I am guilty of being a little creepy, I'm sure. I thought I was doing the right thing to protect my brother. I knew he had something to do with all of this...I just couldn't prove it. I thought if I could just scare her off, then everything would be okay. She would stop looking, stop poking around. I couldn't prove Jack had anything to do with this but I knew that if he did...she would find out.

I guess I have always known that he is not normal...that he hurts people. I have asked him. I have accused him. He has never once admitted to me that I was right. I started to think I was crazy...that I had dreamed up the conversation when we were fifteen years old and he told me he wanted to kill

252

someone. Has he been killing this whole time? I shudder at the thought. No matter what he has done, he is my brother, and I love him. I don't think anyone in our family has ever said that out loud. I know he loves me too; it's just unspoken in our family. I'm sure he's going to clear this whole thing up soon and I will get out of here. Right?

Even as the question enters my head...I know he will never confess to his crimes.

He will let me rot in prison the rest of my life, with no remorse at all.

Chapter Sixty-Four: Riley Morgen

I hate to admit that my mother was right, but she was right. Don't tell her. Soon after coming home from the hospital, I booked my first appointment with a therapist specializing in post-traumatic stress, specifically in law enforcement and military members. Apparently, the therapist served in the military... Army, I think. So, I'm told she will be able to relate to my experiences in some sense. I'm excited to finally start doing what I came to Bearpoint to do... find myself again. I think in law enforcement, or hell just life really, you find yourself helping everyone else around you. Sometimes, you forget to help yourself.

I plan to start my own business...really, just me being self-employed. I'm going to get my private investigator license soon and hopefully find myself in something interesting again. But next time, with much more sleep. Deputy May asked me to join the Bearpoint Sheriff's Office, but I declined. I don't know if small town policing is for me. My heart will always be with the wildness that comes out of policing in a city. Besides, I'm ready to start a new chapter.

Derek May and I sit on the front porch of my cabin, gently swinging back and forth in the rocking chairs facing the mountains. Both of us have a cold beer bottle in hand, silently enjoying the first peace we have felt in a while. I glance over and notice a small piece of medical tape sticking out of the sleeve of Derek's shirt. A small reminder of the bullet that grazed his skin. Everything we have gone through feels so

254

long ago, so far away, as we sit here peacefully. It is hard to believe everything that came from the simple act of finding a necklace on Binkin Trail.

I stand from my rocking chair, the chair swinging back and forward, lightly thudding against the back of my legs.

"Do you want another beer?"

"I shouldn't. I appreciate it though, Miss Riley."

"Oh, the sheriff can't be seen getting drunk with his voters now, huh?" I tease.

"I'm not the sheriff, yet. We'll know when the votes finish comin' in."

I roll my eyes. Sure, why would the citizens of Bearpoint elect the deputy who uncovered the heinous acts of the monster dressed as their previous sheriff? The deputy who took a bullet while taking that ogre down and saved six women who were tortured and abused, one missing for as long as two years? Yeah, nobody wants a hero like that as their sheriff.

"Okay, Sheriff May. I'll get you some tea, then we'll head down to the sheriff's office and wait for the results."

Chapter Sixty-Five: Jack Bennett

I knew my brother would prove his worth eventually. It certainly took him long enough. But I guess I'll forgive him for making me wait. His arrest will help me offload a number of bodies and abductions, freeing me from the possibility of those crimes ever coming back to me. My father seems to see it all the same way, even without us discussing it beforehand. Everything just fell perfectly into place. It's all so brilliant, really. I wonder if the saint understands that he shares a face with the devil now. Minus a scar, of course.

The Minwall detective questioned me and my father separately for hours. We never deviated from the story that we created all those years ago. I was fifteen years old when my old man called me into the den, saying he needed to have a serious talk with me. It was a week after I found out I was just like him...I was not ill or wrong; I was just like my father. He explained to me that even through there is nothing wrong with us, we need to have a story to tell the police if anything ever happened. An alibi. A just in case. Most people will not understand us, so we must be ready for their judgements. He described the camping story to me in detail. He added so many elements and stories, I remember thinking he was being overly cautious. I would never remember all this. We talked about this same story every so often for the next fifteen years. By the time I had to tell it to anyone wearing a badge, I knew it all so well, even I believed it was true. It had become a real memory for me...not some bullshit my father told me to feed the police. It also helped that he has had the camping gear and equipment to back up that story in his truck for fifteen years. He has always understood me, always had my back in all things.

I told Brady so many times throughout our lives to just take my words as truth, to never meddle in my business. He just wouldn't listen. I tried; I really did want him to just listen and go about his pathetic life unbothered. It would have been much easier on everyone involved. I can't say that I love Brady, but he is my brother. He is an obligation in my life, one that I was willing to protect, under specific guidelines. Guidelines that he just could not seem to follow. I don't know that he ever really wanted to be in this family. The whole twin thing is incredibly helpful of course, but really, his downfall here was having that damn scar near his jaw. The scar I gave him when we were sixteen and I was yet to master my knife skills. I will never forget my father's advice… "There needs to be something to distinguish the two of you on the outside, something Brady can't hide from. One day, you will use that to your advantage. One day, you will need it. He is my son, but he is not one of us, Jack.". It made it so easy on me. Some simple scar wax, makeup and a little practice. Suddenly, I am undeniably Brady to anyone who happens to see me conducting my business.

Since then, I have always worn the scar when I abduct or kill. More of an insurance thing than anything else. I had no real plans to ever pin anything on Brady…it was more just an option, a just in case shit hit the fan. I wasn't decided until he refused to stop meddling. He refused to stop pushing and questioning and enticing that cop, Riley Morgen. He brought

257

all of this on himself. I won't even pretend to feel bad about it.

I perfected the scar and took Brady's vehicle while he slept, picked up that whore with the sole intention of ending her. Anger surged through my veins so heavily, burned so deeply...I may have purposely driven past city cameras. He needed to go. I wanted to kill him initially...I almost did. It would have been easier, more satisfying, honestly. But I am a man who is always in control. Even through my anger, I knew this was an opportunity. One that was just too good to pass up.

So, thank you brother, for finally playing your role in this family. It's about damn time.

My phone rings and I glance at the screen. A smile curls my lips and I exhale a deep, relaxed breath.

Ahh, back to business.

Acknowledgments

First and foremost, I want to say thank you to my husband, who has supported this dream before I ever dared to make it a reality. When I was ready to leave comfort and jump into the unknown full force, you acted as my parachute and your support never wavered. Thank you for waking up every day and just being you.

To every police officer who puts on the uniform and fights through the struggles that no one talks about, thank you for your service and dedication. Please don't ever fight your battles alone. This is a brother and sisterhood that values strength in unimaginable darkness…we need to remember that reaching out for help is never a weakness, but instead the greatest strength you can muster.

To every reader, THANK YOU! Thank you for spending your hard-earned money and using your precious free time to support this book! Authors would be nothing without readers, and the gratitude I have for each of you is endless.